SPECIAL MESSAGE TO READERS

This book is published under the auspices of

THE ULVERSCROFT FOUNDATION

(registered charity No. 264873 UK)

Established in 1972 to provide funds for
research, diagnosis and treatment of eye diseases.
Examples of major projects funded by
the Ulverscroft Foundation are:—

* A new Children's Assessment Unit at
Moorfield's Hospital, London.

* Two operating theatres at the
Western Ophthalmic Hospital, London.

* A Chair of Ophthalmology at the
University of Leicester.

* The establishment of a Twin Laboratory at the Royal
Australian College of Ophthalmologists.

You can help further the work of the Foundation
by making a donation or leaving a legacy. Every
contribution, no matter how small, is received
with gratitude. Please write for details to:

THE ULVERSCROFT FOUNDATION,
**The Green, Bradgate Road, Anstey,
Leicester LE7 7FU, England.
Telephone: (0116) 236 4325**

In Australia write to:
THE ULVERSCROFT FOUNDATION,
c/o The Royal Australian College of
Ophthalmologists,
27, Commonwealth Street, Sydney,
N.S.W. 2010.

DOCTOR KNOWS BEST

When Casualty Sister Megan Jones becomes a patient in her own department at the County General, the short shrift she receives from bossy new consultant Giles Elliott is quite a revelation. Then, when he starts trying to reorganise her already efficient system, Megan becomes all the more convinced that, despite his insistence to the contrary, Doctor doesn't always know best!

ANN JENNINGS

DOCTOR KNOWS BEST

Complete and Unabridged

LINFORD
Leicester

First published in Great Britain

First Linford Edition
published October 1994

British Library CIP Data

Jennings, Ann
    Doctor knows best.—Large print ed.—
Linford romance library
I. Title II. Series
823.914 [F]

ISBN 0-7089-7607-7

Published by
F. A. Thorpe (Publishing) Ltd.
Anstey, Leicestershire
Set by Words & Graphics Ltd.
Anstey, Leicestershire
Printed and bound in Great Britain by
T. J. Press (Padstow) Ltd., Padstow, Cornwall

This book is printed on acid-free paper

1

MEGAN JONES wriggled uncomfortably on the stool in the cubicle of the casualty department. She had been waiting for simply ages, first to have her wrist X-rayed and now for someone to come and decide on the treatment. The delay was even more annoying as she knew perfectly well what to do herself because she was Sister of the very same casualty department during the day herself. Just my luck, she thought moodily. When I have an accident there is nobody I know on duty!

The SEN was someone she had never seen before and could only assume had been sent down from the 'bank' reserve of nurses. The Senior House Officer for the night was a locum and her friend Sister Moore was off on a tea-break.

Restlessly she got up and, picking

up her X-rays, clipped them on to the wall-mounted X-ray screen and switched on the light. She could see her wrist looked perfectly normal, so the pain must mean it was just a sprain. If someone doesn't come in a moment, she vowed, I'll put a support bandage on myself!

"There is no point in looking at something you don't understand, young woman. Sit down." The words were uttered in a deep masculine voice tinged with more than a hint of annoyance. At the same time she was firmly and unceremoniously plonked back on the stool by a tall, dark-haired man.

"I . . . er," began Megan, startled into breathlessness by the suddenness of his entry into the cubicle.

"Be quiet," commanded the stranger. "I am a doctor. Just answer my questions. I want to find out whether or not you have done yourself any other damage."

Another locum I suppose, thought Megan, beginning to feel angry at his high-handed treatment of her — and an arrogant one to boot!

"I am perfectly all right," she said stiffly. "There is no need to concern yourself."

"What are you wasting everyone's valuable time for then?" he demanded. "Presumably you thought there was something wrong, otherwise you wouldn't have come in!"

She glanced up at the man towering over her, not used to men so tall. She was small herself and found she had to look up to the doctors, but none of them was as tall as this man. He must be six foot two if he's an inch, she thought, and if he wasn't so angry and bad tempered he could be rather nice looking. At that particular moment, however, his strongly marked brows were drawn together in a frown and his piercing blue eyes looked at her severely. His firmly sculptured mouth was also set in a resolutely disapproving line as he surveyed her.

Megan tilted her head defiantly and

pushed back her cloud of dark, unruly hair with her left hand. The movement caused her to wince with pain, a fact which he immediately noticed.

"Apart from your wrist," he asked, "have you got pain anywhere else? I gather you sustained this injury while you were dancing."

"Yes, I was in the . . . " she was going to tell him that she had been rehearsing for the Christmas revue and that she was a day sister in the casualty department, but she didn't get the opportunity.

He interrupted her brusquely. "I haven't got time for long explanations now, just answer my questions. Have you got pain anywhere else?"

Megan shook her head mutely. There was something completely over-whelming about him, some force that demanded obedience, and Megan, much against her will, found herself responding to it. Wryly she reflected that he might have been the head of the department from the way he was behaving, and not just the locum which he must be.

"Hmmm," he mused, looking at her carefully. "What about your arms and legs? Everything mobile?"

Silently Megan wiggled one foot after the other. "I think I just need my wrist supported," she said eventually.

"I'm the best judge of that," he replied, raising his eyebrows at her. For a brief moment something like a smile flickered in his eyes. "Doctor knows best, remember that!"

It was with difficulty that Megan contained herself. Pride forbade her to tell him she was a trained nurse, for it would look too much like boasting. So she remained silent but inwardly seething as she held out her left hand towards him for inspection. "Ouch!" The protest came out involuntarily, against her will, as he gently flexed her wrist.

"Humph," he snorted, "Just as I thought. You can't go rolling about on the floor without doing some damage to yourself."

"I was *not* rolling about on the floor," interrupted Megan indignantly.

"What exactly would you call it then?" he enquired, his strong fingers gently examining her left wrist. "I thought the whole object of dancing was to stay on your feet!"

"I . . . well, I," Megan hesitated, then laughed. "I suppose it is difficult to describe it any other way." Then she glanced up at the X-ray. "I haven't broken anything, have I?" she asked.

"How do you know?" he countered.

"I can see from the X-ray," said Megan, beginning to feel indignant again. "All I need is a support bandage."

"I disagree — you need more than just a support bandage. You need a cold compress to check the effusion."

Megan opened her mouth to protest, then closed it again. She might as well acquiesce, it was obviously going to be easier that way in the long run.

So she sat as patiently as possible while he went to organise the cold

6

compress. The SEN could easily have put it on for her, but he had sent her away and obviously Sister Juliet Moore had not come back, or if she had, she was busy elsewhere. Megan thought of all her friends who by now would be tucking into a Chinese meal at the local restaurant. If it wasn't for this high-handed locum, she reflected, she would have been on the way there herself. The more she thought about it the hungrier she became!

He came back with a tray and an ice-cold compress. As he deftly bandaged her wrist Megan furtively studied him. She judged him to be about thirty-five or six and his crisp dark hair had just the faintest sprinkling of silver at the temples. His strong features were attractive in a dominant sort of way, and he wore his expensively tailored suit beneath his white coat with a casual self-confidence.

Yes, she thought, watching him carefully; quite an attractive man altogether. She gave a mental smile at the thought of his female patients. Most women tended to go weak at the knees over their doctors anyway, and she could just imagine the effect *he* would have on them. It was strange though, he didn't seem the type to be a locum — he looked more like a Harley Street consultant! Still, it just shows, she thought — appearances can be very deceptive.

When he had put on the compression bandage to his satisfaction he stood up. Megan stood up too and slipped her arms into the sleeves of her coat which he held out for her.

"Thank you," she murmured, turning to face him, raising her eyes to his as she started to button her coat.

For a split second his hands lingered on her shoulders, then suddenly his piercing blue eyes sparkled with a thousand blue lights and a smile spread across his face, revealing attractive, even white teeth.

Unaccountably Megan's heart did a quick flip. The sudden magnetism of his smile unnerved her. Hey girl, she said to herself, don't be ridiculous. This man is only a locum, here today and gone tomorrow. Also he probably has an elegant wife to go with that elegant suit he's wearing, plus four or five children tucked away at some expensive boarding school. In spite of the fact that he was only a locum she instinctively felt that his background was expensive and elegant.

"Thank you for your attention," she heard herself saying stiffly, feeling suddenly shy. At the same time she was telling herself not to be so stupid. It was ridiculous to feel suddenly so ill at ease when all the time he had been glowering at her and being rude she hadn't worried in the slightest. Now, after one brief smile, she felt flustered, like a jittery schoolgirl.

"Do you have far to go?" he asked, his deep voice echoing the smile in his eyes.

"No," said Megan quickly, "I live very near." She didn't tell him how near. Just across the road in fact, in the nurses' block!

"Well, goodnight then," he said, swishing back the curtains of the cubicle and ushering Megan out. "Next time you go dancing, be more careful."

Again she was tempted to tell him what she had really been doing, but he had turned away and walked across to the desk at the side of Casualty. He picked up some notes and Megan could see from his absorbed expression that he had already forgotten about her.

Slowly she turned and walked out of Casualty. It wasn't too late, so she would go and join the others and have something to eat. She knew her friend Susan North would be most upset if she didn't. As she walked down the road towards the restaurant she thought about the mysterious doctor in Casualty. A brief meeting and one flashing smile had left her with a strange, nagging ache. How can someone you've only met for half an hour have an effect on you? she thought crossly. Pull yourself together, you're behaving like a lovesick girl out of a romantic novel!

When she arrived at the restaurant Susan came bustling over and her chattering jerked Megan back to reality with a bump. Susan North had been Megan's friend since they had trained together and she worked with Megan at the County General on the orthopaedic ward. A lively girl, full of fun, it was always good to be with Susan because she enjoyed life to the full.

Susan and the other girls were half-way through their meal and, while she waited for her own to arrive, Megan related the events of the evening to them.

Susan's eyes were as round as saucers as Megan regaled them with the tale of the overbearing but attractive locum in Casualty.

"Do you mean to tell me you went through all that and never even told him that you were a Sister in Casualty?" she demanded. "Honestly, Megan, you are

11

the absolute limit!"

Megan laughed. "He didn't give me the opportunity. He wasn't at all friendly — quite the reverse in fact, and I could hardly get a word in edgeways."

"I should have made an opportunity," retorted Susan, adroitly picking up bamboo shoots and eating them with her chopsticks.

"You weren't there, otherwise you would know what I mean," said Megan. "Anyway, I'm not going to waste time talking about him because I can see my food arriving, and I'm starving!"

The rest of the evening was spent in catching up with all the hospital gossip and it was quite late before the party of girls walked back together to the nurses' block.

The next day the weather was awful and the morning cold and miserable. A penetrating drizzle poured from the skies, making even Megan's umbrella virtually useless. For some reason her spirits felt as low as the depression that was causing the melancholy weather as she made her way to the casualty department to begin the day's work.

Before she had even taken off her cloak Megan knew it was going to be one of those days. Every cubicle in Casualty was occupied and the waiting area was packed to overflowing with an assortment of people, none of whom looked seriously ill. They ought to be sitting in their GP's surgeries, not here in Casualty thought Megan irritably, as she heard the cardiac arrest team being summoned to meet an incoming ambulance.

The morning was chaotic and all the administrative things she had planned to do in the office had to go by the board. Her time was spent helping to get the many and varied patients sorted out, tactfully helping the two senior house officers, who were both new. So it was with some exasperation that she went in answer to a peremptory summons from the Nursing Officer in charge of the accident and emergency services.

Tapping briefly on the door Megan entered briskly. "Mrs Smithson, I hope this won't take long. Casualty is in absolute chaos this morning and I . . . "

"Why, have you been dancing again, Sister?" enquired a sarcastic sounding male voice. The voice had a distinctly familiar ring to it.

Megan spun round to face the tall stranger of her brief encounter the night before. Instinctively she touched her still-bandaged wrist.

"How is the wrist, Sister?" he enquired.

"Much better," she faltered. "But who are . . . ?"

"Sister, you surely haven't forgotten that our new Casualty Consultant, Mr Giles Elliott, is starting today? I sent you a memorandum at least two weeks ago, and in it I asked you to be here at one o'clock today in order to meet him." The Nursing Officer, Mrs

Smithson, sounded aggrieved.

"Oh," Megan gasped, her hand flying guiltily to her mouth. "I had completely forgotten."

Mrs Smithson tutted with annoyance and out of the corner of her eye she saw Giles Elliott give an amused smile. Megan felt her cheeks flaming. He must think I'm an incompetent fool, she thought crossly. "Casualty has been extremely busy this morning," she began.

"No need to apologise, Sister, I do understand," cut in Giles Elliott smoothly. "Although I would appreciate it if you could spare me five minutes of your precious time to show me around." His voice had a sarcastic ring to it which annoyed Megan intensely.

"I can spare you as long as you like, sir," she replied icily.

"What about all those patients needing your tender loving care? Surely they will suffer if I take up too much of your time?"

Angrily Megan glowered at him. It

seemed she could do nothing right as far as he was concerned. Although sorely tempted to snap back, she resisted the urge and maintained a discreet silence. The only outward sign of her seething emotion was her rigidly straight back as she walked quickly down the corridor, the tall figure of Giles Elliott beside her.

"I understand your name is Sister Jones," he said as they walked down the long polished corridor.

"Yes," replied Megan briefly. "Most people just call me Sister."

"What is your first name?" he persisted.

Megan glanced at him uneasily. His face wore an enigmatic expression. Was it polite chit-chat, or was he really trying to be friendly, she wondered? There was no way of telling, either from his expressionless handsome face or the silky tone of his voice.

Deciding it was almost certainly the former, Megan answered rather abruptly, "It's Megan." At that point they arrived at the entrance to Casualty so that put an immediate end to chatting, social or otherwise.

Megan took him on an extensive tour of the department, introducing him to as many staff as possible. To her surprise, far from being aloof and stand-offish as she had expected him to be, he seemed genuinely pleased to meet everyone and was interested in everything they had to say. By the end of the tour round the department it was way past the time when Megan should have had her lunch.

Giles Elliott looked at his watch. "I believe you are late for lunch, Sister," he remarked casually.

"Well," Megan hesitated, "yes I am, just a little." She wondered how on earth he knew what time her lunch hour was scheduled to be.

He obviously noticed her slightly puzzled expression for he said quickly, "Mrs Smithson told me your lunch time." Then he added, "Perhaps we could lunch together. There are still one or two things I would like cleared up, mostly concerning the procedures you have here in this casualty department." He paused and looked at her expectantly.

Megan shifted her weight from one foot to the other uneasily. She didn't relish the thought of suffering an uncomfortable lunch hour with Giles Elliott. She always regarded her lunch-break as sacrosanct, the one time in the day when she could relax properly. The last thing she wanted was to be bombarded with questions about the casualty department while having her lunch.

"I would be extremely grateful, Sister. We'll go now, shall we?" Put like that there wasn't much she could do about it!

Dominating male, thought Megan irritably, straightening the sides of her uniform self-consciously as Giles Elliott flashed her the same devastating smile that had unnerved her the evening before. Expecting me to jump

18

to attention at his slightest whim she thought, although nevertheless she found herself involuntarily smiling back at him.

"That's better," he said with a laugh when she smiled. "At least I can imagine you are enjoying lunch with me, even if in reality you are thinking what a bore it is to be asked questions."

"Oh no, I wasn't thinking that at all," said Megan hastily. Liar, she said to herself silently as they made their way through the maze of long corridors towards the canteen.

It was late, nearly two o'clock, so all the hot food had gone. The choice was extremely limited; pork pie and salad or chicken and salad. They both chose chicken even though Megan knew from past experience that the chicken would almost certainly be as tough as old boots

"I wonder if the chicken here is any better than at my last hospital," he remarked as they took their seats at an empty table by the window.

"I sincerely doubt it," replied Megan truthfully with a laugh. "I must warn you that it is usually quite a challenge to the digestive system. It never fails to amaze me how chicken can be turned into something with the texture of leather."

"It takes years of practice as a hospital cook," he replied, echoing her laugh.

Actually, Megan enjoyed her lunch more than she had anticipated. The conversation flowed easily and apart from giving him the low-down on Casualty she also found out a little about him. He had been a senior lecturer in a large London teaching hospital, but had decided to switch from an academic career to a clinical one, and for that reason had moved out of London.

"I missed the daily contact with patients," he said. His father had been a Harley Street consultant he told her, and he still had the family house in

Cheyne Walk although his father had died. So I wasn't so far out about you, Megan thought with satisfaction. I knew you had that expensive air about you.

"Wouldn't you prefer to do the same as your father?" she asked. "It's very hard work here, for not nearly as much money."

"I know that," came his reply. "I don't need the money, and I certainly don't need the private medicine." There had been a finality about his tone of voice that precluded her from asking any further questions.

It was as they left the canteen that Megan's brother Richard came hurrying by. He was a third-year medical student and had just started the clinical part of his training. "Hi, Megan," he shouted as he zoomed past, white coat flying out untidily behind him. "Don't forget our date — eight o'clock tonight. Hope your wrist is OK."

Megan laughed. "I hadn't forgotten," she replied. She was about to inform

Giles Elliott that she had been roped into the medical student's Christmas revue, but the words got stuck in her throat when she saw the very disapproving look on his face.

"He is a little young, isn't he?" he snapped.

"Young?" echoed Megan in surprise and with a burst of indignation. She supposed his disapproving look was on account of her brother's untidy appearance. "He is twenty," she said. "In fact he'll be twenty-one in January."

"Really?" replied Giles Elliott in a strange voice. "And how old are you?"

"That is a very personal question," retorted Megan, really vexed by this time. She was twenty-six, nearly twenty-seven, but she didn't think that it was any business of his.

"You are right, of course." His voice cut across hers sharply. "It's none of my business. Let's get back to work, shall we?"

His previous friendliness seemed to

have vanished like a puff of smoke. I thought it was women who were supposed to have moods, thought Megan, feeling a little disgruntled at his mercurial change of attitude. He strode along the never-ending corridors back towards Casualty, Megan practically having to run to keep up with him.

By the time the afternoon had come to an end and five-thirty had arrived, Megan was heartily sick of Giles Elliott, the casualty department and everyone in it. In the morning he had been all sweetness and light, but in the afternoon he had swept through the place like a hurricane. Nothing anyone did was right; the two senior house officers were trembling in their shoes and the pupil nurses were so nervous that they started dropping things at the mere sight of him.

Megan kept her temper with difficulty. Outwardly she remained cool and calm, encouraging her nurses and dutifully making notes on all the procedures Giles Elliott wanted changed.

"What's the new consultant like?" asked Sister Moore who was coming on duty for the evening shift.

"High and mighty," replied Megan through clenched teeth. "He thinks he is God's gift to medicine. I really can't think how we ever managed to treat any patients successfully before we had the services of the marvellous Mr Giles Elliott."

"Sounds as if you had a bad day," observed Sister Moore. She was a comfortable, middle-aged woman who had returned to nursing, working in the evenings and nights only, to supplement the family income. "Don't be too hard on him, it's probably a case of the new broom."

"Don't be too hard on him!" exploded Megan. "He has reduced everyone else to the verge of hysteria! That's not the way to get the best out of one's staff." She flung her thick navy blue cloak around her shoulders angrily and, picking up her bag, marched purposefully out of the department.

"Goodnight, Sister," came a familiar male voice behind her. "Enjoy your date."

"I'm sure I shall," replied Megan coldly, looking over her shoulder briefly to acknowledge him. "Goodnight." As she continued down the length of the corridor towards the exit by the side of the out-patient fracture clinic, she was keenly aware of the fact that his piercing blue eyes were following her progress along the corridor. And as she turned the corner towards the exit she saw, out of the corner of her eye, that he was still standing outside his office.

He looked strangely alone and Megan was almost tempted to wave goodnight to him. Don't be ridiculous, she told herself. Don't feel sorry for him, he is probably planning another assault course for you to overcome tomorrow! So with a defiant toss of her dark curls, which somehow always managed to escape from underneath her cap, she turned the corner without acknowledging the fact that she had seen him still standing there.

During the rehearsal for the Christmas Revue that evening, Megan found it difficult to concentrate. Her mind kept returning to Giles Elliott, even though she determinedly did try to concentrate on the work. When she reflected on his behaviour that afternoon in an unemotional way, she had to acknowledge that everything he had said was right. The department had got a little slack, for there had not been a consultant in charge since the previous one had retired nine months earlier. Having been saddled with two completely green senior house officers had not helped much either. Normally there was one experienced SHO to show the new one the ropes, but this year . . . Megan sighed. Perhaps she should have explained that to him.

Mentally she gave herself a shake, Oh well, no use worrying about it, she thought resignedly — tomorrow is another day. Her normally cheerful spirits bubbled to the surface as she threw herself wholeheartedly at last into the rehearsal.

Rather reluctantly she allowed herself to be persuaded into participating in a saucy sketch which involved playing the part of a patient, very provocatively dressed in brief bra and pants. The idea was that every night the students would drag one of the senior consultants up from the audience and on to the stage, and make him plaster her leg. The plaster of Paris bandage would be "doctored' so that it embarrassingly fell to pieces when he tried to use it and Megan's role was to flirt outrageously with the consultant and make his task even more difficult.

They practised it and Megan didn't mind too much. It was all good fun, and she knew from past experience that, however much they protested, the senior consultants were always flattered at being hauled out of the audience. They knew when they bought their tickets that there was more than a fifty-fifty chance that they would actively participate in the proceedings before the evening drew to a close.

By the time the rehearsal finished it was way past midnight and Megan was glad that she had brought her car and not walked or caught a bus. They had been using the lecture theatre at the medical school which was about four miles away from the hospital in the centre of the city. On arrival back at the hospital she parked her ancient little Mini in the car park nearest to the nurses' home and started to walk briskly towards the tower block.

It was an intensely cold night. Her breath was like puffs of steam in the bitterly cold air as she blew on her fingers in a vain attempt to keep them warm, wishing she had had the foresight to have worn some gloves. The first frost of winter tonight she thought, stepping into the pool of light at the entrance to Casualty. Because it was so cold she decided to take a short cut to the nurses' home, which meant crossing in front of the department entrance. The large red letters, CASUALTY, illuminated by the floodlights, stood out clearly, a signpost to anyone needing treatment.

She had just started her walk across the forecourt where the ambulances drew up when, to her astonishment, she saw the obviously very weary figure of Giles Elliott come out. He turned up the collar of his overcoat and hunched his shoulders against the biting cold of the night air. Megan started. Surely he couldn't have been working continuously since she had left at five-thirty? Slowing her stride she hung back, hoping he wouldn't see her, but he did almost immediately.

"You're not going to get much sleep tonight, Sister," he remarked. Megan thought his voice sounded tired but friendly — or was the friendly part her imagination?

"Oh, I've been at rehearsal," she heard herself explaining. "It's the medical students' revue and I've got roped into it." She laughed. "I must need my head examined, getting involved with that crazy lot!"

"I suppose that young man who spoke to you at lunch-time is in it," he said.

"Oh yes, of course," replied Megan enthusiastically. "He is one of the leading lights."

"I can imagine," came the wry reply. Then, to Megan's consternation, he put his hands either side of his head on his temples.

"Are you all right?" she asked hesitantly. On a sudden impulse she hurried forward and put her hand on his coat sleeve.

He smiled and she noticed how exhausted he looked, with lines of weariness etched into his face. "I'm just a little tired, that's all," he replied. "A nasty accident came in, and I felt I just couldn't leave one inexperienced senior house officer with a case like that. The other registrar was tied up in theatre with a surgical emergency from one of the wards, so there was no one to help him."

Reaching across suddenly with his other arm he took her hand, which had been resting lightly on his coat sleeve, and clasped it. "My word, your hand is cold," he said softly. "Perhaps I should burst into song and sing 'Your tiny hand is frozen'!"

His voice held a joking note, almost teasing, but his eyes were clouded and looked into Megan's large brown ones seriously. She looked away quickly as her heart gave an unpredictable lurch, and she could feel it beating uncomfortably loudly against her ribs. The warmth from his large hands sent strange tingling sensations throughout her whole being. She was conscious that she had never reacted to anyone in that way before.

Megan gulped self-consciously, then tried to laugh lightly as she said, "You know what they say, cold hands, warm heart."

"And is it?" he asked in a low voice.

"Is it what?" asked Megan, unable to tear her gaze away from his magnetic blue eyes.

"Is your heart warm?"

"Well, I . . . er," Megan felt her cheeks burning in spite of the cold night air. "I really don't know," she mumbled.

He laughed and released her hand. "We are both tired and mustn't stand here talking all night," he said. Then he added, "I was only teasing, you know. I wasn't expecting a confession on the state of your heart.

"Yes, I mean . . . yes, I know," stammered Megan. "Goodnight."

She sped on her way back to the nurses' home, a strange warmth pervading her being. At the same time she was cursing herself for behaving like a dumbstruck sixteen-year-old, just because he had held her hand.

2

THE next morning passed fairly uneventfully, at least as far as Giles Elliott was concerned. His piercing blue eyes seemed to be everywhere and observe everything, but Megan noticed thankfully that he wasn't in such a fearsome mood as the one he had been in the previous afternoon.

"I was dreading this morning," confessed Jamie Green, one of the senior house officers. "Yesterday I couldn't put a foot right, but today he has actually congratulated me for reading an X-ray correctly!"

He and Megan were busy in one of the cubicles, cleaning and dressing superficial lacerations on the legs of a ten-year-old girl who had taken a nasty tumble from her bicycle.

"Perhaps he's still tired after last

night," said Megan. Then she grinned mischieviously at Jamie. "We had better be thankful for small mercies! There's no knowing when he'll strike again."

"How is this young lady?" A familiar deep voice behind her made Megan jump. She and Jamie exchanged guilty glances, both hoping their conversation hadn't been overheard.

Giles Elliott picked up the casualty card lying beside the patient and quickly scanned the brief notes. "Hmm, I see you fell off your bicycle," he said to the little girl.

"Yes," she whispered, her eyes wide and dark against the pallor of her face. "Mummy will be cross, I'm not supposed to ride on the road."

"Where is Mummy?" he asked gently, noting that there was no parent's signature on the card.

"She is on her way in," Megan replied for the little girl. "We had to telephone her at her workplace. She had already left for work before

Amanda here decided to ride her bike to school."

"I see," he said slowly. Then he smiled reassuringly at the anxious little girl. "You have been very lucky indeed — all you have got are some grazes and bruises. So if you promise me that you won't ride your bicycle again on the road, at least not until you are older, I'll try and persuade your mother not to be too angry."

"I promise," whispered Amanda, smiling at him gratefully.

Huh, your charm works on women of any age, thought Megan, watching him. He only had to smile and the child responded to him in much the same way Megan herself had responded. The only difference is *you* should be old enough to know better, Megan told herself.

As far as Amanda's mother was concerned, there was no need to worry. She was so glad to see her precious daughter in one piece that there were no recriminations for her breaking the rules. However, Giles Elliott made a point of emphasising that Amanda had promised him she wouldn't ride her bicycle on the road again. At least, not in the foreseeable future. Mother and daughter left the casualty department, the little girl's legs swathed in dressings as she held on tightly to her anxious mother's hand.

Giles Elliott stood beside Megan watching mother and daughter as they made their departure. "That's the problem of latch-key children," he said with a sigh.

"Yes, I suppose it is a problem," agreed Megan. "But if you are divorced, like Amanda's mother, a single-parent family trying to cope with work and a child, there is no alternative, is there?"

"No," he agreed, a grim look on his face.

Something puzzled Megan. He seemed to take it almost personally, almost as if it was his own worry, but before she had time to dwell on these thoughts something happened that put the whole episode completely out of her mind.

A man in his middle fifties had come in with a sprained ankle — not a particularly bad sprain but it did need a support. After all the routine questions had been asked and his ankle had been X-rayed and examined by one of the junior doctors, Megan left a student nurse, who had plenty of experience, to put on the supporting bandage.

She was standing at the desk by the side wall opposite the patients' cubicles and was about to call in the next case, when the cardiac arrest signal went off on her bleep. Even as she turned around, before she heard the automatic voice over the bleep system, she saw that the man had keeled over, falling from the couch to the floor, pinning the young student nurse beneath him. She had obviously had the presence of mind to push the cardiac arrest button as they both fell.

For once everything went with clock-work precision. The anaesthetist on call happened to be in Casualty at that moment, so there was no delay in intubation, and after only half an hour a resuscitated patient, stable enough to be moved, was being wheeled up to the coronary care unit for observation.

Megan turned her attention to the student nurse. "Are you all right?" she asked anxiously. "I'm afraid there wasn't much time to enquire before."

The girl gave a nervous laugh. "Yes, I'm OK, but I must admit that I do feel a bit shaky now that it's all over."

"You go off and have a coffee now," Megan told her. "You look as if you could do with a break. Take a friend with you, we can manage without two of you."

"Are you sure?" the student hesitated.

Megan looked around Casualty. All was quiet for the moment. "See for yourself," she said. "Take your chance now, while you can. We may not be as quiet as this for the rest of the day!"

It was only after they had gone that Megan realised Giles Elliott hadn't been there when the arrest had happened. Pity, she thought ruefully, he would have seen us at our most efficient.

Jamie Green was sitting at the desk looking at some X-rays on the wall-mounted screen and Megan wandered over to him. "Pity our new consultant, Mr Giles Elliott, wasn't around to see our efficient arrest team in action," she remarked.

Jamie pulled a face and gave a resigned sigh. "Yes when everything goes with textbook precision there is never anybody to see it. Not anybody important, anyway." He raised his eyebrows expressively. "But when something goes wrong, you can be sure you hit the headlines!"

"That's one of the hazards of medicine — the criticism is far faster in coming than the praise." Giles Elliott had walked up behind without either of them hearing him.

Megan turned round quickly, feeling slightly irritated. He seemed to make a habit of looming up into conversations. It was irrational of her, she knew, to feel that way, particularly as he had been very pleasant. It was just that the sound of his voice made her jump and inexplicably sent her heart into a crazy erratic rhythm — and anyway, she told herself, trying to ignore the beating of her heart, she wasn't too keen on having a consultant looking over her shoulder, particularly when the consultant concerned noticed everything!

So her voice had a slight edge to it as she said, "Excuse me, gentlemen, I have work to do in my office. Now seems like an ideal time to do some catching up on my paperwork."

As she walked past the now empty cubicles in Casualty and back to her office, she could almost feel Giles Elliott's piercing blue eyes boring holes in her back. Once in her office, instead of getting on with her paperwork as she should have done, and there certainly was a mountain of it to do, she sat staring with unseeing eyes out of the window to the car park outside. The little alarm on her watch emitted a tiny high-pitched bleep, reminding her that it was on the hour. She glanced at her watch. Good heavens, twelve o'clock already. She had promised to meet her brother that day for lunch at one and that gave her only an hour in which to make some headway into the paperwork she disliked.

Sighing, she pulled the overladen tray towards her. This was one of the Sister's tasks she hated, but it had to be done. And, with a tremendous effort, by the time one o'clock came she had managed to make quite a sizeable inroad into it. So it was with a sense of well-earned relief that she pushed the tray away and set off to meet her brother.

On arrival at the canteen she could see Richard with some of his friends already seated inside. Hastily grabbing a salad lunch she queued up to pay for it, then joined her brother.

41

"Sorry I'm late," she said, squeezing in beside him. "I was trying to get some paperwork out of the way."

Richard grinned cheekily. "I still think the efficient Sister image doesn't suit you," he said.

Megan aimed a friendly blow at him which he successfully managed to dodge. "I can't say I can imagine you being a dignified doctor," she countered. "What useful work have you been doing this morning?"

"Well, for a change we actually did something very useful," answered one of Richard's friends, Simon. "We laid out and numbered the specimens for a first-year anatomy spot test. I call that being very useful."

"Oh well, in that case perhaps you can answer a question for me," came a voice from the far end of the table. It was Rupert Grimes, a first-year medic whose elder brother was a third-year, hence the fact that he was lunching with them.

"Fire away," said Simon with all the

self-assurance of a third-year medical student, feeling infinitely superior to a first-year.

"What was the point of having that frog as item number four?" asked Rupert plaintively. "Was the Prof purposely trying to catch us out?"

At the mention of the frog, eight pairs of incredulous eyes swivelled down towards the end of the table where Rupert was sitting.

"Did you say frog?" Simon's voice rose in a disbelieving squeak.

"Yes, *frog*," repeated Rupert even more plaintively. He consulted a scrap of paper. "Yes, specimen number four, I've got it written down here."

"That wasn't a frog, you fool," burst out his brother. "That was a bladder! My God, you're going to do well if you can't even identify pickled specimens!" The end of his sentence was lost in the great gale of laughter that suddenly swept around the table.

Poor Rupert blushed a shade of beetroot red from the roots of his hair to his neck. Megan felt sorry for him, but even she couldn't help laughing helplessly along with the rest. At last the laughter subsided and he shrank down in his seat, trying to look as inconspicuous as possible. Megan took her handkerchief from her uniform pocket and wiped her streaming eyes, and as she did so she suddenly sensed, rather than saw, that she was being observed.

Almost as if she were a puppet on a string she felt her head turn in the direction of the gaze. Her large brown eyes, still sparkling with laughter, met the steelcold disapproval of ice blue ones. Giles Elliott stood, tray in hand, regarding the hilarity at the table with a distinct air of disdain about him. Hostility surrounded him like a physical aura.

Megan felt her hackles rise in annoyance. What right had he to look so damned supercilious? She was off duty, for the moment anyway, and could laugh with whom she pleased.

Defiantly she tilted her chin, flashed back a look of equal disapproval from her expressive brown eyes and turned her back towards him. Later she saw that he was sitting at a table with some very elderly consultants, and she couldn't help feeling a little touch of satisfaction when she saw he was looking decidedly bored.

Serves you right, thought Megan, knowing full well through the hospital grape-vine that the particular consultants he was sitting with had only one topic of conversation, money. Apparently, so it was rumoured, they had the private practice at the local nursing home sewn up between them. Well, they had nothing to fear from Giles Elliott, if what he had told her earlier was anything to go by, and he certainly had little in common with them. They were all years older than him.

Megan left the canteen, avoiding meeting his eyes as she walked past his table, and made her way back to Casualty. The afternoon passed quickly.

A succession of minor accidents were admitted, some patients arriving under their own steam, others being picked up from road traffic accidents and being brought in by ambulance. But there was nothing serious, just cuts and grazes, sprains and a broken arm — enough, however, to keep all the staff constantly on the go. Then a little boy was brought in by his mother with a plastic bullet lodged up his nostril. He had well and truly shot himself up the nose as he had been playing with a toy gun!

Giles Elliott was called and decided to attempt to remove it in Casualty to avoid unnecessary trauma by admitting the toddler into a hospital ward, and he asked Megan to assist him. After a few moments, though, he laid down the nasal forceps and turned to her.

"It's too firmly lodged. Get an ENT surgeon down to have a look, will you? I think he will probably need to be admitted and have it removed under a general anaesthetic."

The ENT surgeon arrived and agreed

with Giles Elliott's opinion. Megan was not sorry to see the back of the rumbustious youngster. It had been quite a task trying to prevent him from swarming under, or climbing up, anything and everything in sight. He toddled away happily, not in the least bit worried, in the direction of the ward area, clutching his mother's hand and with the plastic gun, the cause of all the trouble, still firmly clenched in his other fist.

"An hour with one three-year-old boy and I feel quite exhausted. It must be old age," said Megan to Giles Elliott with a laugh. Then she added, "Would you like a cup of tea? I have a kettle and a teapot in my office."

"Yes I would, Sister. I'll be along in five minutes." His answer was positive and immediate.

As she was making the tea Megan wondered what on earth had possessed her to ask him to her office for tea, especially after the way he had glowered at her at lunch-time! However, she took great pains with the tray, setting it out carefully with the best cups she kept for special visitors and putting some chocolate fingers on to a small side plate.

Giles Elliott knocked and came in, his tall frame seeming to fill every spare inch of the room. "This is nice," he said, settling in the armchair reserved for her visitors, stretching out his long legs in a relaxed fashion before him.

Suddenly Megan found she was ridiculously nervous and it was with a great effort that she poured the tea and milk and passed him the sugar, feeling that if she relaxed one iota the cup would clatter uncontrollably around in the saucer.

Giles Elliott sipped his tea appreciatively, watching Megan's slim figure in her dark blue Sister's uniform, her trim waist emphasised by the wide belt with its silver buckle, her cloud of unruly dark hair caught up in an attempt at a severe bun. "I like you better with your hair down," he said suddenly.

Megan blushed, her long dark brown lashes fluttering on to the delicate curve of her cheeks. "I have to make an effort to look efficient," she replied as coolly as possible, "even if sometimes I'm not."

"Really? From what I've seen you appear to be extremely efficient. Sister Moore, the night sister, seems to be excellent too."

Megan raised her expressive brown eyes to his, momentarily pausing in the process of pouring herself a cup of tea. She was amazed — she had been thinking that he disapproved of the way everything was organised.

He laughed, accurately reading her expression. "Just because I might grumble a little doesn't mean to say that I don't like the way things are done here. In fact, I think they are done very well."

"Grumble a little!" Megan interrupted without stopping to think. "You were absolutely dreadful yesterday. You had everybody shivering in their shoes!" Even as she spoke she could have bitten out her tongue — it wasn't the politest thing to say.

But Giles Elliott didn't seem to mind. On the contrary, he laughed again. "I didn't notice you shivering in your shoes," he said. His deep voice had a teasing note to it.

"I'm not the shivering-in-the-shoes type," replied Megan, unable to resist the impulse to smile at him. She finished pouring her tea and made to move to sit behind her desk.

"No, don't sit there, sit here," he commanded, indicating the chair beside his. "If you sit behind your desk I shall be the one shivering in my shoes; I shall feel as if I'm being interviewed."

This time Megan laughed out loud disbelievingly. "Now, if there is one thing I am certain you would never do," she said, "it's that you wouldn't shiver in *your* shoes for anyone."

He smiled. "You're right," he

acknowledged. "We are two of a kind in that respect." He patted the chair beside him again. "So come and sit here and we can chat for five minutes, then I'll examine your wrist. I see you have the support bandage on. Good girl."

Megan perched uneasily on the chair next to him. He crossed one long leg over the other in a completely relaxed fashion, but she felt anything but relaxed. Quite the opposite, in fact. The proximity of his masculine presence was distinctly unnerving. She felt him looking at her and reluctantly she felt the power of his gaze drawing her eyes to his. She raised her large brown eyes to meet his blue ones. The blue of his eyes seemed strangely dark and his intent look was almost hypnotic. Unaccountably Megan's throat felt dry and she swallowed nervously as he ensnared her with his gaze.

"Megan," he said softly, "tell me something."

"Yes, what is it?" She heard her voice

answering him and it sounded miles away, as if it belonged to somebody else. The unfathomable expression in his eyes was sending unfamiliar feathery ripples along the length of her spine, ending in a sinking feeling in the pit of her stomach. The teacup was held unheeded in her hand as a feeling of bewilderment engulfed her. Her heart beat rapidly out of control and her pulses raced violently. If I feel like this when he just looks at me, what would I feel like if he kissed me? The thought crossed her mind fleetingly.

He lowered his eyes and took another sip of his tea, breaking the spell he had held over her.

"Do you mind if I call you by your first name?" he asked.

Megan felt vaguely surprised. It was not the question she had been expecting, but then on the other hand she was not really sure what she had been expecting.

"No, of course not," she tried to answer in a matter of fact tone, making sure that all her wild imaginings of the previous few moments were not reflected in her voice.

"And you must call me Giles," he said. He finished his tea, eased his long frame out of the chair and stood up. "How about coming out to dinner with me tonight?" he asked. "Unless, of course, you have a regular male friend who would strongly object."

"No, I don't have any particular boyfriend," answered Megan quickly, surprised at his invitation, "but I'm afraid I do have another rehearsal for the medical students' Christmas revue."

"Oh yes, the Christmas revue." Was it her imagination or did that disapproving look fit across his face again?

"I know you may think it's a bit silly, and it probably is, but it does provide a lot of people with some well-earned laughter," she heard herself saying defensively.

"I didn't say I thought it was

silly," he replied, raising his eyebrows expressively.

Megan stood and took his teacup from him. "You didn't have to," she answered. "It was written all over your face."

"I see," was all he said, but his voice held a pensive note. Then, as Megan started to open the door for him, he stopped. "One moment — I was going to look at your wrist, wasn't I?"

"Oh . . . really, there is no need," faltered Megan, his closeness sending those delicious shivers up and down her spine again. Hastily she put her bandaged wrist behind her. "It's quite all right," she muttered.

"Doctor knows best," he said, an amused glimmer in his blue eyes as he reached a long arm around her to grasp her bandaged wrist.

Megan's heart stopped in its tracks, or at least for a moment she thought it had. His dark face was so close to hers and the steely blue of his eyes still had that enigmatic colour, a dark warm colour evoking thoughts of passion. Megan swallowed hard, her throat dry. She felt herself swaying towards him and involuntarily she parted her delicate pink lips, craving to feel the warmth of his firm mouth on hers.

It was with an enormous feeling of anticlimax that she watched him as he took the bandage from her wrist. Fool, she told herself fiercely, just because he asked you out to dinner, and just because his eyes are a fascinating shade of blue, doesn't mean that he is interested in a little nobody like you. Be sensible. A wealthy, handsome man like him must have plenty of women in tow. He's probably married, anyway, and just has nothing to do this evening.

He, for his part, kept his head lowered while he made a careful and thorough examination of her wrist, so she was unable to see his expression.

"Thank you," she said stiffly when he had finished. "Thank you also for your invitation. I'm sorry I had to decline."

"Are you?" he answered wryly, opening the door to her office. "Some other time then, perhaps."

"Yes, that would be nice," replied Megan non-commitally. She busied herself needlessly with the teacups, anything to avoid catching his disturbing gaze again.

"I'll say goodbye for today," he said. "I have a consultant's meeting to attend now and you'll be off duty by the time it is finished." He paused in the doorway. "I hope you enjoy your rehearsal, Megan."

"I'm sure I shall," answered Megan, but the words sounded hollow in her ears. She would have much rather gone out to dinner with him instead. "Goodnight," she added as an afterthought.

"*Giles*," he prompted.

Against her will Megan was forced to look up. Even though physically now they were separated, the look from his blue eyes still sent her pulses racing. "Giles," she repeated slowly, being rewarded by that sudden devastating smile that did dangerous things to her heart.

After he had gone she stared at the cream-painted wood of the door pensively, wondering about him. He seemed such an unpredictable character. Stand-offish one moment, friendly the next, but above all physically attractive in the extreme. Megan knew that she had to be very careful; it would be easy to fall in love with a man like Giles Elliott.

No point in allowing yourself luxurious thoughts like that, she told herself firmly. He's almost certainly married and only asked you out because he has just moved down here from London and left his family up there. The more she thought about him, the more she realised that, apart from knowing he had a beautiful house in Cheyne Walk, she knew absolutely nothing else about his personal life.

Try as she might she simply couldn't concentrate at rehearsal that evening. "Megan," grumbled Richard, "you are hopeless tonight."

"I know," apologised Megan guiltily. "I'm sorry, I'm rather tired and I'm finding it difficult to concentrate."

She was very pleased, therefore, when the rest of them decided to call a halt earlier than usual, and she declined an offer to go with them to the students' bar. Sometimes she went for Richard's sake, but it always made her feel positively geriatric, all the students were so young.

However, although she had declined Richard's offer, Megan felt restless and not in the least bit like going back to her minute flat in the nurses' block. As she hadn't seen Susan since their meal together she decided to take a chance and call on her. It would be someone to have a gossip with.

Turning up her coat collar against the cold, and digging her mittened hands deep into her pockets, Megan hurried along towards the tower block after she had parked her car. She had completely forgotten that Susan was still unaware that the stranger she had thought to be a locum had turned out to be the new Casualty Consultant at the County General. On arrival at the tower block she made straight for Susan's flat, and to her delight Susan was there and feeling as restless as Megan.

"I know," said Susan, "don't take your coat off. I'll put mine on and we'll go up to the Woodpecker for a drink. Do us both good to get away from here."

Megan agreed. Somehow the small rooms of the tower block flats seemed extra claustrophobic that evening. The two girls made their way out of the hospital grounds and up the steep hill towards the hospital local, the Woodpecker. Megan told Susan about Giles Elliott, although she omitted to mention the fact that she thought he was extremely attractive, and she certainly didn't mention that her heart did strange things whenever he came near her!

"What is he like?" Susan demanded to know.

"A real stickler for perfection when it comes to work, I can tell you," replied Megan. "He put the fear of God into everyone on his first day, but he seems to have eased off a little since then. Now that he has finally realised that we are not all complete imbeciles," she added.

"I must find some excuse to come down to Casualty," said Susan. "I'm dying to see this man. Fancy you being treated by your own consultant!" She went into peals of laughter at the thought. "You were his first casualty from the County General, only he didn't know it at the time."

Megan laughed too. "Yes, I suppose I was," she said. "I don't suppose he has thought of that."

Pushing open the door of the pub they entered into its welcoming warmth, a gratifying change from the sharp cold of the frosty night air. The first sight that met their eyes was a couple of senior registrars they both knew well, seated at the bar on the tall stools. One was a Canadian, an anaesthetist called Johnny Cox, and the other was a surgeon named Martin Taylor. They had both been at the hospital for about three years on their senior registrar rotations, and both were the sort of characters who became well known to everyone. Loved by some, disliked by others, but known to everyone!

"Hi girls, what a sight to gladden sore eyes." Johnny's loud Canadian twang echoed around the half-empty bar. "Here we were, just the two of us, wondering what two handsome fellows like us were going to do on our own and lo and behold, two gorgeous girls like you turn up!"

Megan laughed. "Flattery will get you nowhere. Why aren't you in the Mess — that's your usual haunt, isn't it?"

"It's run out of beer again," said Martin, heaving a sigh. "Our wretched Mess treasurer keeps forgetting to pay the brewery."

"Don't tell me the brewery doesn't trust the junior doctors, and won't deliver until they have been paid," teased Susan.

"Too damned right they won't," said Johnny ruefully. "But now that you two have turned up, it has made my evening. I don't care if the Mess has no beer, I like it better here." He put his arm round Megan and gave her a resounding kiss on the side of her cheek. "What can I buy you to drink?"

"Stop it, you idiot," Megan laughed, pushing him away. She knew him too well to be offended. Then she turned to Susan. "We might as well resign ourselves to the fact that we are not going to have a quiet natter by ourselves."

"Who cares?" said Susan, climbing up on to the stool beside Martin. "I was feeling like a change this evening anyway. We'll have a red wine each," she said to Johnny, answering for Megan as well as herself.

The four of them decided to move so that they could talk more easily, and changed over to a table in the corner where they sat munching crisps, drinking and exchanging hospital gossip and jokes.

"I hear the students have roped you into their revue," said Johnny to Megan. "I can't wait to see it. A little bird has told me we are going to see quite a lot of you!"

Megan blushed. "Johnny, how did you know that?" she demanded. "It's supposed to be a secret."

Johnny slung his arm loosely around her shoulders. "If there is one thing I like, it is a woman with a beautiful body," he crooned into her ear.

Megan ignored him. He was the hospital gigolo, a different girl every night, quite harmless as long as no one took him seriously. "Johnny, I've known you too long to be taken in by you," she said severely.

He gave an exaggerated sigh. "You're a hard woman, Megan," he replied.

The conversation continued between the four of them in the same bantering vein for the rest of the evening until the landlord called for time. The two men rose and started to usher the girls out. It was as they were on the point of leaving the warmth of the bar for the cold night air outside that Megan was suddenly aware that Giles Elliott was there. He was sitting at the far end of the bar, slightly in the shadow, but from his position he would have had a full view of the four of them at their table.

Megan raised her hand, intending a brief friendly salute, but it wavered and died as she encountered his stony, anything but friendly stare.

"Goodnight . . . " She tried to say the name Giles, but it stuck in her throat, so she left it at the brief goodnight.

"Goodnight, Megan," came his icy

reply. "I'm glad to see the rehearsal went well."

Before Megan could reply, the others, who hadn't seen him, or wouldn't have known who he was if they had, dragged her out into the cold night.

"Come on," said Johnny, shivering as he linked arms with the two girls. "Let's quick-march, it's damned cold out tonight."

Martin caught hold of Megan's arm on the other side and the four of them marched off together briskly in step down the road, back towards the glow from the complex of lights marking the hospital site.

Fleetingly Megan looked over her shoulder in time to see Giles Elliott emerge from the Woodpecker. He stood unmoving in the doorway, staring after their retreating figures. Then suddenly she realised what he must be thinking. He must have thought she had lied to him about the rehearsal when she had told him she couldn't go out to dinner. Suddenly she felt utterly miserable. He must think very badly of me, she thought unhappily. I must make sure I explain to him tomorrow. The icy sarcasm of his voice as he had said, "I'm glad to see the rehearsal went well," echoed round and round inside her head. Remembering his lonely figure standing in the doorway she wished more and more she had had the chance to explain to him.

"Hey, Megan," teased Johnny, "why so silent? Have you seen a ghost?"

Megan smiled and didn't answer him. No, it was not a ghost she'd seen but a man who had come so suddenly into her life only a few days ago, and now seemed to be a disturbingly integral part of it.

3

TO Megan's chagrin she didn't see Giles Elliott at all the next day. Apparently he had gone to London to some special conference on trauma, and had taken one of the senior house officers with him. Megan found this out because an orthopaedic registrar had come down to the casualty department for the day to help out during the other junior doctor's absence.

The fact that she couldn't explain to Giles Elliott why she had been in the Woodpecker the previous night and not at rehearsal, bothered Megan more than she cared to admit to herself. She felt restless and edgy and it was only with a supreme effort of self-will that she concentrated on her tasks. The mere fact that she found it so difficult to put him out of her mind bothered her too, and eventually she became annoyed with herself. This is ridiculous, she told herself severely. Stop making mountains out of molehills; the man probably hasn't given you another thought since last night. However, try as she might, Giles Elliott's face with its stony stare of disapproval kept floating in front of her mind's eye.

To make matters worse, at least as far as Megan was concerned, the department was unusually quiet, with no major casualties, no emergency admissions. In fact, by the middle of the afternoon there was absolutely nothing to do. The orthopaedic registrar took the opportunity to do some reading for his final FRCS which was coming up soon and the nurses stood around after they had tidied everything in sight and made sure all the trolleys were fully stocked with everything necessary.

Megan could have done some more paperwork, something she always hated, but this particular afternoon she just knew she definitely would not be able to concentrate on anything as mundane as that. So, commandeering a couple of pupil nurses, she decided to reorganise the store cupboard.

Once they had got stuck into the job there was no stopping her. She changed everything around, labelled the shelves, got them dusted and cleaned, and then they set about the task of restacking the shelves.

The store cupboard was quite large and unfortunately for Megan and the two pupil nurses it had a radiator in it. It had once been intended for use as an office, but due to some oversight on the part of the hospital architect, there was no ventilation or window. The young nurses struggled to turn off the radiator at Megan's request, but couldn't manage it. Megan had a try too, but was equally unsuccessful, so they carried on working in the rather hot and stuffy room. The net result of which was that by the time they had finished the task all three of them looked hot and flushed and extremely dusty.

Megan glanced at her watch as they placed the last box of plaster-of-Paris bandages on the shelf. It was five o'clock, time for the pupil nurses to go off duty. "OK, you two can go now," she said briskly. "Thanks for all your hard work."

"Are you sure everything is done, Sister?" asked one of the girls.

"Yes, thank you," replied Megan, standing with her hands on her hips looking about at the reorganised cupboard with satisfaction. "I'll just write a note and pin it on the door asking the cleaners to give the floor a good wash, and that will be that. So off you go, and thank you."

The two girls needed no second bidding, flying off down the corridor, chattering non-stop, towards the female changing rooms.

Megan felt tired now, but at least she had worked the thoughts of Giles Elliott out of her system. Absent-mindedly she ran a hand across her forehead, pushing back the rebellious dark hair that had escaped from beneath her cap during her exertions. In a few moments Juliet Moore would be coming on duty, just time for her to write the note for the cleaners.

As she closed the door of the store cupboard behind her and stepped into the corridor, Megan suddenly became aware of two piercing blue eyes, with more than a hint of amusement in them, regarding her. She was also palpably aware of her very dishevelled appearance. Half-heartedly she tried to straighten her cap and push her hair back in place, acutely conscious of his blue eyes taking in every detail of her appearance. She felt her cheeks burning with embarrassment and knew she was turning crimson.

"Have you been having an orgy in the cupboard, Sister? If so, I'm very sorry to have missed it. I should have stayed here instead of going up to London!"

"I, we . . . um . . . " If Megan was flustered before, he had completely unnerved her now, and to make matters worse he took a step nearer. Involuntarily she took a step backwards and ended up leaning against the store cupboard door. Her luminous brown eyes, fringed by their impossibly long lashes, looked panic-stricken as she unexpectedly felt herself falling backwards. The door to the store cupboard had not been fastened properly and the light pressure of her slim young body had been enough to send it flying open and her tumbling backwards. Hitting the floor with a thud that knocked all the air out of her lungs, Megan lay still for a split second.

"Megan, are you all right?" Giles' large frame was bending over her, lifting her gently to her feet.

Still dazed and bewildered, Megan clung to him, vaguely conscious of the comfortingly rough texture of his tweed jacket and the pervading masculine smell of his skin, with its faint, lingering perfume of aftershave. His face was so close to hers it would have been easy to reach up and kiss that strong, determined jawline, and Megan found herself terribly tempted to do just that.

Common sense prevented her. Instead she said, rather lamely, "I've been clearing out the store cupboard."

He smiled down at her. "You seem to make a habit of falling over. What part of your anatomy have you damaged this time?"

Self-consciously Megan tried to push him away. Nothing," she said firmly. "I'm sorry, it was a stupid thing to do."

"Yes, it was rather," he replied, his blue eyes smiling. He made no effort to release her — if anything, it seemed to Megan that his arms tightened around her a little.

Her long lashes fluttered down over the becoming curve of her high cheekbones as she lowered her gaze, unable to meet the searching blue of his eyes any longer. "I'm all right now," she muttered quickly. "Thank you very much for picking me up." It seemed a rather inadequate thing to say but she couldn't think of anything else. In fact she found it difficult to think at all with his arms around her.

"Don't mention it," came his low reply. "I really quite enjoyed it."

"You did?" Megan's head came up in surprise and simultaneously his dark head came down to meet hers. She was briefly aware that he had kicked the cupboard door shut behind him before his lips came down on hers, blotting out everything. His mouth was hard and demanding, and Megan's natural instinct was to respond to the urgency of his kiss. A confusing mass of emotions spun like stars in her head.

Abruptly he let her go, saying, "That is what happens to young women who fall at my feet! You have been warned!"

Megan looked at him suspiciously. He was laughing at her.

"My goodness, Sister, you look as if

you have never been kissed before," he said. Now he was laughing out loud.

"Not in a store cupboard," replied Megan stiffly, unsure which had unnerved her most, his kiss or his laughter. She tried to muster as much dignity as possible. "Personally I think it's much too stuffy in here for that type of activity." She made to go past him, trying to reach the door.

His hand snaked out in a quick, agile movement, grasping her slender-boned wrist as she tried to reach the door knob. "Sorry, I shouldn't have teased you," he said, but his blue eyes were still laughing.

Vainly Megan tried to wrench her wrist from his grasp, but against the strength of his long, strong fingers her ineffectual struggles made no impact at all.

"Tell me," his voice was low, throbbing with a vibrancy that caused Megan's senses to reel, "where *would* you suggest for this type of activity?"

Her cheeks burned a fiery pink

with the red-hot flush that swept across them. Damn the man, he was purposely embarrassing her! Indignantly her brown eyes flashed fire.

"It's been a long day and I'm tired — and I am *not* in the mood for jokes." She tilted her small oval chin defiantly. "If you will please open the door for me . . . " The tone of her voice was severe and self-composed. Quite the opposite, in fact, of the way she was really feeling.

He took the hint and courteously released her, opening the door for her at the same time. Megan marched out with as much dignity as she could muster in the circumstances, and went straight to her office without so much as a backward glance. Once in her office, however, she rushed to the small mirror that hung on the wall, standing on tiptoe in order to see into it.

Quite what she was expecting to see she wasn't sure. Irrationally she expected a different girl to gaze back at her from the mirror. The fact that she had been briefly, but thoroughly, kissed by Giles Elliott made her feel different. Hesitantly she raised her hand and gently touched her lips, the lips that only a few moments ago had been kissed. He may have been teasing, but Megan knew that somehow, for her at least, their relationship would never be the same again.

For the umpteenth time since she had met him, she wondered about him. Was he married? Did he have a girlfriend or maybe even a fiancée? She could imagine the sort of girlfriends he would have. Elegantly casual in expensive classic camel coats, with beautiful leather shoes and handbags. Not like herself in the least, having to search around the shops to find fashion that suited the meagre pay of a hospital sister.

Megan sighed. Put all thoughts of him out of your head, she told herself. He is not going to look at a scruffy little thing like yourself, who has to stand on tiptoe to look in the mirror!

His type of girl is tall and svelte, one of those Sloane Ranger types you're always reading about.

Her dreaming thoughts were abruptly halted by the arrival of Juliet Moore. "Busy day?" she enquired, looking curiously at Megan's flushed appearance.

Self-consciously Megan tried to straighten her cap yet again, and turned away from Juliet to take her cloak off the hanger on the wall. "No, very quiet indeed. If you are thinking that I look a bit . . . "

"As if you have been pulled through a hedge backwards, to be specific," interrupted Juliet, laughing.

Megan gasped and went over to the mirror again. "Oh, do I look as bad as that? Whatever must Giles think?"

"Oh," said Juliet, a note of interest creeping into her voice, "Giles, is it?"

"He told me to call him Giles," said Megan defensively, "and the reason I look like this is because I have spent the afternoon reorganising the store cupboard. Thanks to me, you will be able to find anything and everything, no matter how much of a hurry you may be in. All the shelves are labelled and everything is in its proper place."

Juliet laughed. "No wonder you look so hot and bothered. For a moment I thought you had been having another altercation with Mr Elliott. I mean *Giles*," she added with a twinkle in her eye. She came across to Megan. "Here, let me put your cap straight. For goodness' sake, you can't go down the corridor like that, you look as if you've been on the bottle!

Megan laughed. "Thanks, Juliet, I can't see in this wretched mirror properly. We'll have to lower it."

"Then I won't be able to see," grumbled Juliet good-naturedly. She towered over Megan. "But we'll lower it — I can always bend at the knees to look at myself." She gave Megan a friendly slap on the shoulders. "Off you go, you look respectable now."

Megan grinned at her. She was a nice, comfortable person, easy to get on with. In some ways it was a pity that they worked different duties and never really had the chance to get to know each other well. Giving Juliet a cheery wave she set off down the corridor. As she passed Giles Elliott's office she noticed the door was open and that he was on the telephone. It was impossible not to hear what he was saying as she went past for the corridor was quiet and empty and his voice had a deep, carrying note to it.

"Of course, darling," he was saying. "I can't wait to see you either. See you at the weekend then — take care."

Megan's heart plummeted straight into the bottom of her sensible flat black shoes. So he did have a girlfriend, or maybe even a wife after all. Anyway, certainly someone he called darling, and someone he couldn't wait to see. Her pace quickened — she wanted to get down the corridor and around the corner before he emerged. She managed it and, letting her breath out in a sigh of relief, wrapped her thick cloak tightly around her and stepped out through the automatic sliding doors into the cold night air.

Thank goodness I don't have to go to rehearsal tonight, she thought. Not many free nights left before Christmas; the revue starts next week, and then it's Christmas week. She was off duty for Christmas and was looking forward to snatching a few days with Richard and her mother. She and Richard had planned to drive down to Devon together.

It was only after she had showered and washed her hair that it suddenly dawned on her that she still hadn't explained to Giles Elliott the reason for her presence in the Woodpecker the previous night. Oh well, she thought, heaving a sigh of resignation, it doesn't matter anyway — he'll be seeing his darling at the weekend!

The telephone in her room rang, the double ring of an internal call. Probably Susan, thought Megan, picking it up.

"Hello," she said, expecting to hear Susan's voice.

"Is that you, Megan?" a deep familiar voice came down the line. Megan's heart skipped a beat. It couldn't be — not Giles Elliott, surely? "Megan?" he said again, a questioning note in his voice.

"Yes, it's me." Megan's voice was hesitant. "Who is it speaking?" Although even as she asked she knew.

"It's Giles here. I wondered if you were doing anything this evening. Do you have another rehearsal?"

"No, I don't," replied Megan. Then she added, for the sake of something to say, "I've just washed my hair."

A deep chuckle came down the line. "At least you can't give me the excuse of saying you've got to wash your hair!"

"Excuse?" echoed Megan.

"Yes, excuse," he said firmly. "Is there any other reason you can think of that will prevent us from going out and having a meal together tonight?"

Megan paused, conflicting thoughts and emotions racing one after the other through her head. "No," she said finally.

"Good," he replied. "I'll pick you up outside the nurses' block in an hour's time." Then the phone clicked. He had put down the receiver without waiting for her reply.

Megan sat still, transfixed, holding the dead phone in her hand. Half of her was pleased that he still wanted to take her out for a meal, the other half annoyed at his imperious assumption that she would acquiesce!

However, she scurried round and got herself ready. She chose one of the dresses she liked best, a jade green woollen dress that clung to the youthful curves of her slim figure and swirled out in graceful folds from the hips. The colour suited her delicate colouring and brought out the hint of red in her dark tresses. Brushing her hair vigorously she wondered whether to wear it down loose or whether she ought to put it up in a chignon. Deciding that a chignon would be more elegant and make her look more sophisticated, she carefully pinned it up.

Putting on her one and only winter coat, a dark brown velvet, Megan picked up her handbag and gloves and left the flat.

She was ready and waiting on the pavement of the perimeter road when Giles' car drew up smoothly beside her. "I hope you haven't been waiting out here in the cold long," he remarked, opening the door for her.

"No, I've only just come out," replied Megan, suddenly feeling shy and self-conscious in his presence.

He laughed. "I think you are too polite. You would have said that even if you had been standing in that freezing wind for ten minutes," he said.

"That's where you are wrong," retorted Megan. "I should have waited five minutes, then I would have gone back inside." She thought for a moment; now seemed a good opportunity to explain her apparent rudeness the night before. She cleared her throat in embarrassment. "I know you think I didn't have a rehearsal last night, even though I said I did because . . . "

"The rehearsal finished early and you went to the pub," he interrupted her.

Megan turned her head sharply to look at him. In the darkness of the car she could just make out the shadow of a smile lurking about his lips. "How on earth do you know that?" she demanded.

"Jamie Green told me today, when we went to London," he replied smoothly. "He also told me that the young man you have lunch with, and who is the leading light of the revue, is your brother."

"Well, yes he is," began Megan. "Why else do you think . . . ?" Her voice trailed away. So that was why he had asked her how old she was! She burst out laughing. "You thought I was cradle-snatching, and that he was my boyfriend!" she said between gasps.

"I did." His voice sounded almost annoyed. "You look so ridiculously young yourself, it would be natural for you to attract younger men."

"Thanks for the back-handed compliment," said Megan drily, "most women want to look younger than they are, but not ridiculously young!"

"Sorry," he said. "That was a tactless thing to say." He turned his head briefly towards her in the darkness. "Anyway, if it's any consolation, you look very elegant tonight, and every inch your twenty-six years."

"Thank you, but I don't need any consolation," snapped Megan, wondering how on earth he knew she was twenty-six — or was it just an educated guess on his part? Unless she asked she would never know, but although she was dying to know whether he had actually taken the trouble to find out, she was damned if she was going to question him. Instead she contented herself with asking, "How did you know where I lived?"

"Easy," he laughed. "If one wants to know anything, just ask the hospital switchboard, the fount of all knowledge where anything in the hospital is concerned."

Megan smiled; that was true. The switchboard operators had fantastic memories, they seemed to be able to remember everything about everyone.

"I'm living in hospital accommodation at the moment which I must say I find rather oppressive, until I find somewhere suitable down here to buy."

"Will you sell your house in Cheyne Walk?" asked Megan.

"No, I don't think so," he replied, swinging the car into the car park of an Italian restaurant. "It can stay as the family house, which we can all use whenever any of us are in London."

At his words something froze up inside Megan. The mention of family, and the word "us' indicated beyond doubt that he must be married. Why then was he asking her out, and why had he kissed her? Did he think she was the type to go out with married men?

Almost as if he had read her thoughts he turned suddenly and said, "I hope you don't mind me asking you out again on the spur of the moment, but I know very few people down here and, as I said, my hospital accommodation is rather oppressive."

"Of course I'm not offended," answered Megan smoothly. "I'm pleased to be able to help. Once you are settled here you'll soon get to know lots of interesting people, and in the meantime I'm not averse myself to getting out of my little flat. I find it oppressive too." She paused. "Perhaps one day, if I'm careful with my money, I'll be able to buy a house of my own to live in."

"Your reply sounds very formal, Sister Jones!" His voice had a teasing note to it which Megan made herself resist.

"It was meant to," she replied, opening the car door and getting out.

"Anyway, you won't have to buy yourself a house," he said carrying on the conversation as he locked the car doors. "You'll get married, and your husband will buy you a beautiful house."

"Not at the rate I'm going," said Megan practically. "Mr Right never seems to come along." She said the words lightly, but her heart was strangely heavy. It had never bothered her before, but now suddenly she felt that her Mr Right never *would* come, because he was right there beside her. The only trouble was that he already had a family — he had just said so.

"Perhaps you are too choosy," he said, taking her arm and leading her into the restaurant.

"Perhaps," answered Megan wistfully, suddenly wishing she had never agreed to go with him for a meal.

Very carefully she kept the conversation light and informal during dinner, determined not to let it get on to a personal level. Soon she had him laughing with her anecdotes of the various characters who worked in the County General.

"I can see it is not only the switchboard that is the fount of all knowledge," he said, smiling at her, his vivid blue eyes sparkling.

Megan steeled her heart to look at him without going weak at the knees, something she found increasingly difficult to do. Why, oh why did he have to be married, her heart cried out, because by now she was convinced that he was.

"You forget I've been at the County General ever since I started nursing. I did my training here and I've stayed here ever since."

"Have you never thought of moving on?" he asked. "Most girls seem to get itchy feet once they have qualified."

Megan sighed and before she knew it she was explaining to him the reasons she had decided to stay put. Her father had been a doctor in general practice in Devon, and had died very young of leukaemia, leaving her mother with an inadequate pension and two young children to bring up.

"The house, our family home, still isn't paid for," she told Giles, "and I feel morally bound to help my mother with the mortgage as she went without so much herself in order to give Richard and me a good education."

"I'm sorry," he said gently, reaching across the table and enclosing her small hand warmly within his large one, "It must have been very hard for you all."

Megan smiled. "Yes, it was, but at least we've got the happy memories. My father was such a happy-go-lucky man. Even when he knew he was dying he refused to get depressed, not even at the end. The only thing that did worry him was the fact that he had not taken out a good insurance, and he knew my mother would have a financial struggle when he was gone."

She sighed again, thinking of those dark days. Then she brightened. "But my mother is a remarkable woman too; she always used to say to him, 'Who needs money? We have our love, that's enough,'"

"She was right of course," said Giles sombrely. "No amount of money is a substitute for love. So, you see, you have been rich really, having a happy childhood, having loving memories to look back on."

He sounded strangely envious. Megan laughed. "You know all about me," she said, "but I know very little about you. All I know is that you have a house in Cheyne Walk."

For a moment he hesitated, then he said slowly, "My childhood was not happy. My parents eventually split up after many terrible rows, and my mother left the country. My sister and I stayed behind in London with my father and had a succession of housekeepers — some good, some bad and some distinctly indifferent." He smiled at Megan. "So you can see I envy you your background, even if it was cruelly shattered by your father's death. As you say, you still have happy memories of your mother and father together. Mine, I'm afraid, are only bitter, and they say history always repeats itself."

With that cryptic remark he changed the subject, leaving Megan more than a little puzzled by his last few words. However, he adroitly steered the conversation on to lighter subjects and soon had Megan laughing with his hilarious accounts of incidents that had occurred at his previous hospitals.

The meal was delicious too. Megan had never been to that particular Italian restaurant before, it was much too pricey for her, but she had certainly heard of its reputation. They started off with antipasto, Parma ham and figs, a combination Megan had never tried before.

"Do you like it?" enquired Giles, anxiously watching Megan's face as she tasted the dish for the first time.

"It's delicious, and so simple to

make. I must remember to do it myself sometime," replied Megan.

They followed this with a plate of gnocchi in a cheesy cream sauce, then duck with orange and sage followed by blackcurrant sorbet drenched in some kind of liqueur. By the time they had finished Megan felt in a distinctly mellow mood, a state brought on by the good food and wine they had consumed, plus the pleasure of being in Giles' company.

"It's just as well I don't come here very often," she remarked jokingly. "I think I would soon put on weight."

Giles looked across the table, his eyes lighting for a brief second on the curves of her slender figure outlined by the jade green dress. "I agree," he said. "You don't want to put on weight, your figure is perfect the way it is."

Megan blushed self-consciously and he laughed. "You look very pretty when you blush," he said.

"It's a habit I wish I could grow out of," muttered Megan.

"Why?" he asked. "I think it is a charming habit."

Megan didn't answer — she lowered her eyes and drained her coffee-cup, aware all the time that his gaze was lingering appreciatively on her. Damn it, she thought nervously, they had managed to keep things fairly impersonal during the whole meal, and now by one chance remark she was suddenly aware again of the crackling undercurrent of electricity between them.

Giles paid the bill and Megan slipped into her brown velvet coat, assisted by an attentive waiter. Then they both walked out of the warm restaurant into the cold night air outside.

"It's so cold I think we might have snow," remarked Giles, taking her arm as they walked over the crisply frosted ground in the silent car park towards his car.

The touch of his hand on her elbow sent delicious prickles of fiery flame along her veins, spreading throughout her whole being. Stop being ridiculous, Megan told herself in panic. He is only politely holding your arm!

She heard her own voice answering him so matter-of-factly it sounded to her as if it was somebody else's voice, echoing from far away. "I do hope it doesn't snow — Richard and I are planning to drive down to Devon for Christmas."

"I shouldn't worry about it," came his reassuring reply.

Once seated in the car, Megan assiduously tried to manoeuvre herself as far away from him as possible. She had the ridiculous feeling that if she brushed against him visible blue sparks would fly!

Giles said nothing; he seemed suddenly strangely silent and remote, almost as if his mind was on other things. Although it was obvious to Megan that he wasn't paying any attention to her, she was still painfully aware of him. The faint odour of his aftershave permeated the car, reminding

her of the moment when he had kissed
her in the store cupboard.

As they drove along in silence she
stole a furtive look at his profile. Even
just looking at him caused her heart to
somersault. There was a strength in his
profile, and yet a tenderness too she
thought, looking at his strong jawline
with its firmly moulded lips.

All too soon for Megan he drew the
car to a gentle halt outside the block
of nurses' flats. The time had come
now to say goodnight and he turned
towards her.

"Thank you for a lovely meal,"
murmured Megan hesitantly. "I enjoyed
this evening, thank you."

"Have you, Megan?" His voice was
soft and low. "I've enjoyed it too.
Thank you for rescuing me from a
lonely evening."

"Don't mention it." Megan forced
herself to keep her voice light and
carefree. But the words died in her
throat as he slowly and deliberately
reached forward and pulled her head

97

slightly towards him.

"I've told you before that I like your hair better down," he said softly as he deftly removed the pins holding it up in the sophisticated chignon. Free of the pins, her hair fell down in a loose, fragrant cloud, and as it did so he ran his long fingers through it, gently kneading the back of her neck.

Megan's heart beat with a loud uneven thud as she sat, mesmerised by the sensual movements of his fingers. Then slowly, so slowly, he pulled her towards him. Their lips met and fused in a moment of indescribable sweetness, his mouth clinging to hers for a magical moment before he drew his head back.

It seemed to Megan an eternity that he held her like that, his eyes looking searchingly into hers through the dim light of the car. Then his lips brushed the tip of her nose in farewell.

"Goodnight, Sister Jones," he said. "Be good," and with a deft flick of his wrist he opened the car door for her and Megan climbed out without a word.

Numbly she half raised her hand in a salute as he pulled away, but he didn't look back. Watching the red rearlights of the large car as it sped away into the darkness, Megan felt deflated and confused.

He had been so gentle, so tender . . . The expression on his face had led her almost to believe that he cared, but then suddenly it was as if it had been wiped off by some invisible hand. The expression that replaced it had been careful and guarded. Suddenly he had become the consultant again as he had formally said, "Goodnight, Sister Jones."

Later that night, as she tossed and turned sleeplessly in bed, Megan realised that she had told him almost everything about herself, but that she still knew very little about him.

"Why don't you just tell me you are married and have done with it?" she said out loud, thumping the pillow viciously. "Why don't you just admit you want a brief flirtation with the little Sister in the casualty department, just to stop yourself from becoming too bored! And what if that is exactly what he does want?" she whispered to herself. "What are you going to do, my girl?"

She didn't really have to tell herself — she knew the answer. She was not the flirtatious type. She was . . . what was it he had said? Too choosy, yes, that was it. She smiled miserably to herself in the darkness of her room. A leopard can't change his spots, she thought, and neither can I.

4

THE weekend came and went in a flurry of last-minute activity concerning the revue, so many things needed to be done before the curtain went up. Megan found herself roped in for more and more jobs, finding an article for the props team, photocopying extra music for the orchestra, even down to hastily stitching costumes on the opening night.

"Thanks, Sis, you're a brick," said Richard, dashing past as she sat huddled in a corner sewing and blowing her a kiss.

Megan glowered at him. "A brick, am I! Well, let me tell you that at the moment that is exactly what I feel like throwing at you. The amount of work you volunteered for me to do!"

Richard pulled a cheeky grimace and Megan smiled back. It was impossible to be cross with him for long, he had one of those sunny dispositions that charmed everyone. She guessed in the years to come he would have every patient eating out of his hand, and probably every nurse too!

Anyway, she didn't really mind all the extra work. She hadn't had a moment when she had been off duty to spare, so Giles Elliott had remained banished to the back of her mind, which suited her just fine. There was no time to dwell on the woman he called 'darling' on the telephone, the one he couldn't wait to see at the weekend. Even during the day there hadn't been much time to think of him. The first really hard frosts of the year had arrived accompanied by a sprinkling of snow, and as usual Casualty has been inundated with minor fractures. At one point there had been seven patients with Colles' fractures waiting in Casualty. Thanks to a speedy anaesthetist using the bier block technique and the efficiency of Giles Elliott, they had all been dealt with and sent home by the afternoon.

Megan was always amazed that the bad weather invariably produced such an influx of accidents. If it was frosty she felt people ought to be expecting it to be slippery and to be extra careful, but they never seemed to take any precautions. It was just the same in autumn when the first leaves fell. The number of motor cyclists who skidded on the leaves and had to be brought into hospital had to be seen to be believed! However, this time she almost welcomed the influx of patients — it gave her a breathing space, a time when she didn't have to think or worry about her emotions where Giles Elliott was concerned. The only things she had time to think about were the patients she was attending to, or the Christmas revue when she was off duty.

The revue, wittily called *Doctorpussy*, opened and proved to be a great success. On the first night when she had to do her scantily clad routine Megan felt terribly embarrassed, but with the audience falling about in the aisles with laughter she soon lost her inhibitions and began to enjoy herself too. All too soon it came to Saturday, the last night of the revue.

The Saturday morning dawned bright and sunny, bitterly cold with a fresh layer of snow, and it was with reluctance that Megan hauled herself from her warm bed. It was the last chance she had of going into town before Christmas, and there was some last-minute shopping she just had to do. It's now or never she thought, wrapping her dressing-gown tightly around her and dashing into the bathroom opposite, getting across the draughty corridor as quickly as possible.

Once in town she trudged through the snow, in and out of the brightly lit stores. There seemed to be a million people there, and all with the same idea. The shops glittered and sparkled with Christmas decorations, the crowds shoved and jostled good-humouredly and the tune of "Jingle Bells' blared from every shop doorway.

Megan was heartily glad when she had made her last purchase and decided to treat herself to a well-earned coffee. She was making her way across a narrow side street towards a small coffee-shop when she noticed the young girl in front of her. The girl wasn't looking where she was going; she was walking along, her bright fair head bent, listening to music from the earphones clipped to her personal stereo.

Megan heard the motor cycle coming but the girl didn't, and nor did she see Megan waving her hand frantically. In panic Megan started to run, but the snow hadn't been cleared in the side street and it slowed her down. The motor cyclist braked, and then everything seemed to happen in slow motion. Megan reached the girl and tried to pull her out of the path of the motor cyclist, but he followed them in an uncontrollable skid, dirty snow splaying out either side of his wheels as he desperately tried to stop.

Afterwards Megan couldn't remember exactly what had happened next, except that she found that both she and the motor cyclist were kneeling in the snow by the side of the girl. She had fallen and was lying with her parcels scattered around her and with one leg twisted beneath her.

"Are you all right?" Megan asked the motor cyclist quickly.

"Yes, I'm OK — the snow cushioned my fall. But what about her?" His face looked grim. "What shall we do?"

"Just help me," said Megan firmly. "I'm a nurse. Everything will be all right, don't worry." She looked at the girl who stared back at her, her bright blue eyes filled with pain and fear. "Don't be frightened," said Megan gently, "Everything will be fine."

"I'm OK," said the girl, struggling to sit up, but as she did so she gave a little scream and fell back.

"I'm afraid you are not quite all

right," answered Megan. "I'm pretty certain you've broken your leg." She turned quickly; by now a small crowd had gathered. "Can somebody please send for an ambulance right away?" she asked. Then she turned her attention back to the injured girl, reassuring her and making her as comfortable as possible in the circumstances.

The ambulance arrived on the scene and soon the patient was lying on the stretcher in the ambulance as it sped away towards the County General. Megan had to endure the police questioning as she was the principal witness, and had no alternative but to tell them that it had been entirely the fault of the nameless young woman.

"Thanks, miss, for your statement," said one of the policemen finally. "We know where to find you if we need you again."

By the time she actually got her very belated cup of coffee Megan felt she really needed it. She sat in the small Italian coffee-shop enjoying her *cappuccino*, its frothy top sprinkled with grated chocolate, and idly wondered who the young woman was. She wondered too how many other cases had gone into Casualty to keep the staff busy, all because of a little extra snow — although in the case of the girl and the motor cyclist, the snow had actually prevented a much worse accident. Silly girl, thought Megan. Someone should have stopped her wearing earphones while she was walking along in the street, or at the very least she should have looked where she was going.

Reluctantly Megan set off through the cold wet snow again to make her way back to the hospital. Just time for a short rest and a bath, then the final night of the revue and the party that followed it.

That night there was much merriment backstage before the revue, but for some reason it made her feel depressed. She hadn't seen Giles Elliott to actually speak to for absolutely ages. She hadn't even seen him at the revue, which was surprising as most of the consultants came.

Megan was ready and waiting in the wings for the opening number when Jamie Green squeezed into his place beside her. He was doing the lights and worked them from a small control board jammed in at the side of the makeshift stage.

"Fancy that about Giles Elliott's daughter," he said, fiddling about with his controls.

"About who?" asked an astounded Megan, hardly able to believe her ears. She had suspected that he was probably married, but even so, Jamie's words came as a terrible shock. A cold splinter of ice went through her heart.

"Yes," whispered Jamie, quite unaware of the havoc he was wreaking on Megan. "She came into Casualty today, knocked down by a motor cyclist apparently. Got off very lightly though — a small fracture of the lower end of the fibula. About fifteen years old and quite an attractive creature too," he added.

"Fair hair?" asked Megan, everything suddenly clicking into place. She had known those bright blue eyes reminded her of someone, and the facial characteristics too, now she thought about it.

"Yes," replied Jamie, looking up in surprise. "How did you know?"

Megan didn't stop to enlighten him as she marched on with the rest of the cast for the opening number. The first sight that met her eyes as she galloped on stage was Giles Elliott sitting in the front row and by his side sat the young girl from the morning's incident, her leg conspicuous in its fresh white plaster.

How she got through the opening number Megan just didn't know. Luckily for her she knew the routine backwards, which was just as well, she reflected later, because she felt so unnerved by the sight of him sitting in the front row that her brain refused to function.

While she was changing for her second sketch Megan mentally reprimanded herself. You knew he would probably come to the revue, she told herself. Be honest you've been hoping he would come. Yes, but not with his daughter, her inner voice wailed in despair. Oh, be sensible, Megan told herself fiercely. You suspected he was married! You've wondered about it — well now you needn't wonder any more; now you know! He *is* married, and he has brought his daughter along to prove it . . .

There wasn't much more time to think before she was due on, this time in her scanty bikini to do the sketch with whichever consultant the boys at the front of house dragged up from the audience. She'd seen the Dean of the medical school also sitting in the front row and guessed it would be him; the students usually involved the Dean on the last night. So it was with surprised horror that she saw it was not the Dean, but Giles Elliott who was being dragged up on to the stage.

Her expression must have shown on her face although Megan thought she was doing a good job of disguising her feelings, for when he got near her Giles whispered, "*I'm* the one supposed to look horrified and reluctant, not you!"

"I . . . I thought it would be the Dean," Megan whispered back.

"Sorry to disappoint you," came the crisp aside.

The sketch commenced and Giles Elliott joined in with an enthusiasm that surprised and disconcerted Megan. All the week she had let her hair down and had enjoyed teasing the consultants, but not when the consultant was Giles Elliott. She felt shy and embarrassed, her cheeks were burning and she was sure her face must be the colour of a beetroot. Gritting her teeth she did the best she could and breathed a heartfelt sigh of relief when the sketch was over and she made her escape off stage.

Richard was waiting in the wings.

"You were a bit off tonight, Sis," he remarked. "I thought you would have given it all you've got on the last night."

"I did the best I could — I'm not out to win an Oscar!" snapped Megan as she scurried past.

Richard raised his eyebrows in surprise at his sister's unusual display of bad temper. Megan, for her part, was sorry she had snapped at him, but her nerves were distinctly frayed at the edges to say the least. All the time the same words were constantly running through her mind, repeating over and over again with a monotonous insistence. He's married, he's married . . . Try as she might, she couldn't banish those words from her mind.

When the evening finally finished and the curtain went down on the revue for the last time, Megan would have given anything to have gone back to her flat and to have drowned her sorrows alone. But it was not to be; she was duty-bound to go to the after-show party, but she determined not to stay too long.

With her face scrubbed of stage make-up and wearing a pair of jeans and a sweater, she was standing rather miserably in a corner with a glass of wine in her hand when Johnny Cox spied her.

He came zooming over in his usual enthusiastic way. "Say, girl, what are you doing in this corner all by yourself? Where have you been all my life?"

"You know where I've been, Johnny," erupted Megan irritably. She really didn't feel like coping with Johnny's extrovert behaviour at that point in time. Johnny, however, totally ignored the fact that her greeting was less than enthusiastic and propelled her vigorously across the room towards a group of people.

"Say, everyone, I have here one of the most ravishing nurses who appeared in the show tonight," he announced to all and sundry. "Miss Megan Jones, tara!" He blew an imaginary trumpet fanfare with his hands and shoved Megan forward into the middle of the group.

Suddenly Megan was aware of the pristine white of new plaster again as she realised that sitting down in the midst of the group was Giles Elliott's daughter, and by her side was the man himself.

"Ah, Miss Jones," he said, his blue eyes sparkling, "perhaps you would care to autograph my daughter's plaster?" He put his arm casually around his daughter's shoulders. "Joanna, can I introduce Megan Jones, Sister in Casualty."

Joanna looked up and the same vivid blue eyes quizzed Megan. Then she smiled. "Daddy, we have already met. This is the girl I told you about, the one who looked after me when I had the accident."

Giles looked at Megan. "Is this true?" he asked.

"Yes, it is," replied Megan. "But of course, I didn't know then she was your daughter," she added quickly.

"No," he rapped. "If you *had*, perhaps you wouldn't have told the police it was Joanna's fault."

"I most certainly would have done," replied Megan, her brown eyes flashing indignantly. "The fact that she is your daughter doesn't alter the fact that the motor cyclist was not to blame."

"I really fail to understand how he hit her," he said. "Surely he must have seen her? Are you certain you saw everything?"

Megan bristled. "Are you doubting my word?" she exclaimed angrily, forgetting where she was.

Joanna reached up and touched her father's arm. "Megan is quite right," she said. Then she heaved a big sigh. "I might as well tell you, because you'll find out anyway sooner or later. I was wearing those earphones you hate so much and listening to pop music."

"As you were walking along?" asked her father incredulously.

"Yes," whispered Joanna in a small voice.

Megan glanced at him; his face was as black as thunder. Suddenly she felt sorry for the young girl. It had been a silly thing to do and now she was paying the price. Impulsively she reached out and touched Joanna's shoulder.

"All's well that ends well," she said. Then she laughed, trying to bring a smile to Joanna's rather worried looking face. "I think we can safely tell your father that you won't be doing it again."

"You bet," said Joanna gratefully, thankful for Megan's intervention. "In fact, if you like, Dad, you can sell them. You can put the money towards that hi-fi I've been wanting," she added cheekily, seeing her father smile.

"I'm sorry I doubted your word for a moment," he said slowly to Megan, adding, "One is always protective towards one's children, you know."

"I wouldn't know," replied Megan a

trifle sharply. "I haven't got any!"

Before Giles Elliott had an opportunity to reply, her brother Richard joined them. He took one look at Joanna and it was quite obvious he liked what he saw. "Can I help you across to the refreshment table?" he asked her.

Joanna glanced questioningly at her father, who smiled and nodded in reply. "Yes, that would be lovely," she responded and off they went, a crutch supporting her on one side and Richard on the other.

"Can I get you any refreshments?" Giles asked Megan.

"No thanks," said Megan shortly. She didn't feel like socialising, least of all with Giles Elliott who had not only turned out to be married, but who had also doubted her word into the bargain.

"Oh, come on," he said in a soft, persuasive tone of voice that caused Megan's heart to churn with bitter anguish. "Do have a sausage roll at the very least."

"It isn't even Christmas yet, and already I feel that if I see another sausage roll I shall scream!" said Megan ungraciously.

Giles Elliott chuckled. "My goodness, if it wasn't so late at night I'd say you had got out of bed the wrong side!"

Megan felt a little ashamed; there was no need to be so churlish with him. After all, he had probably assumed that she had realised he was married all along and he didn't know what romantic fantasies she had been weaving around him. "I'm sorry," she said. "I know I seem bad-tempered. I'm tired, that's all."

"Come with me," he said, grasping her arm firmly and steering her across the room. "I know the Dean has some rather more exciting bottles than those which are out here, reserved for consultants and wives only."

"But I'm not your wife," protested Megan.

"No, but you're my friend, and that's good enough," he replied. So Megan found herself squashed into a small side room with a large balloon glass of brandy in her hand. Giles clinked his glass with hers. "Better?" he asked.

Megan stared down at the golden brown liquid eddying around the glass. Was it better or not? She wasn't sure. Why, oh why does he have to be married, nagged the voice at the back of her mind. The brown eyes she raised to his were troubled, but her lips smiled as she stifled the thoughts and said, "Yes, much better thanks." She touched her glass merrily against his and took a huge gulp of the fiery liquid.

The Dean, Professor Smithson, came across. "Pleased to meet you, my dear," he said to Megan. Then he winked. "I envied this chap here, I can tell you," he nodded at Giles. "But I was pleased to see that our newest consultant joined in the spirit of things."

Megan blushed at the embarrassing memory. "I don't know how I ever let myself be talked into doing that sketch," she said.

"I'm very glad you did," said Giles, his blue eyes dancing. "It isn't every day I get the chance to lay my hands on attractive young women!"

"Quite, quite," said the Dean, absent-mindedly pouring himself another brandy and then wandering off clutching the bottle to his ample front.

"I think that's the last you've seen of the brandy," said Megan, glad of an excuse to change the subject.

"I'm sure you're right," replied Giles with a rueful smile. "Come on, let's go and find out what the rest of the party is doing, and I'll see if I can find you something more exciting than a sausage roll. Maybe there is some caviar."

"And maybe there isn't," replied Megan, laughing at such a notion.

The party was in full swing, the disco blasting out music at an ear-splitting level. They found Richard and Joanna sitting in a corner chatting, Joanna with her leg resting on two chairs.

"Daddy," she exclaimed when she

saw them coming, "Richard has invited us down to Devon for Christmas. He has rung his mother, and she says she would be delighted. I've said yes — is that all right?"

Megan stared with amazement and horror at her brother. What ever could have got into Richard? Fancy inviting Giles Elliott, his wife and daughter to their home for Christmas! Whatever must he be thinking of?

"But what about your mother? She must be asked," she said to Joanna, voicing her thoughts aloud.

"Well, what about her?" replied Joanna looking surprised. "She won't be coming." Then, seeing Megan's obviously puzzled look, she laughed. "Sorry, I thought you knew. Daddy and I are quite alone this Christmas, nobody at the house in London and a horrible hospital flat here. I've been moaning about it to Richard and he said you lived in a big house by the sea."

"We do," replied Megan, wondering where on earth Joanna's mother, Giles

Elliott's wife, was. "But we shall only be having a very quiet Christmas, rather an old-fashioned one."

Joanna clapped her hands with glee. "That's just perfect," she said, "I've never had an old-fashioned English Christmas."

"Perhaps Megan would prefer Christmas with just her own family," interrupted Giles. "Just because you are enthusiastic, my dear, you mustn't forget other people's feelings."

Joanna's faced dropped a mile. "Oh no," she said. "I hadn't thought of that. It was silly of me, I'm sorry."

"Of course I don't mind," said Megan quickly, not really knowing what else she could say, "and I know my mother will be absolutely delighted. She likes nothing better than cooking. It will be the perfect excuse for her to cook mountains of food." Acutely aware of Giles Elliott's questioning gaze on her, she forced a bright, if somewhat brittle laugh. "The only thing is, you will have to promise to eat every single thing she cooks."

"I will," said Joanna, her eyes shining, "and Richard has said he may take me up on to Dartmoor to see the meet of the hunt on Boxing Day."

"So that's settled then," said Richard with satisfaction. "All we've got to do now is to organise the travelling arrangements. I was going with Sis, I mean Megan," continued Richard turning to Giles, "but if you are coming too perhaps I could take Joanna down a couple of days before, as I shall be free then, and you could bring Megan when you both get off duty on Christmas Eve."

"Richard," interrupted Megan sharply, "I'm sure Mr Elliott has got plenty of things planned to do before Christmas. He is a very busy man."

"Nonsense, I'm not that busy," answered Giles, "and for goodness' sake don't call me Mr Elliott! Joanna, I know, would love to start her holiday early." He raised his eyebrows quizzically at Megan. "Unless, of course, you have any objection to driving down with me? I can assure you I'm quite a safe driver."

"No, I don't have any objection," Megan was forced to admit, "it's just that . . . "

"Then it's agreed," interrupted Giles, raising his glass in a salute to her. "Let's all drink to our Christmas together."

Dumbly Megan raised her glass in a toast. There was nothing she could do; it was a *fait accompli* and that was that. It would have looked very bad-tempered and ungracious to have tried to protest. So it was agreed that Richard would drive Joanna down the following Wednesday in Megan's little car, and Giles would bring Megan down on the Friday afternoon, which was Christmas Eve.

Richard, with Joanna hobbling at his side, went off to the students' bar, leaving Giles and Megan alone.

"Do you mind?" he asked, coming

straight to the point. "I know you were rather bulldozed into the arrangement."

Megan lowered her expressive eyes uncomfortably. Did she mind? How could she say to him that if he wasn't married she wouldn't mind at all — in fact she'd be over the moon? But no, she thought wryly, you certainly can't tell him that! So she said instead, "No, of course I don't mind. Why should I?"

"I just thought you didn't seem overenthusiastic, that's all," came the reply.

"I . . . I was surprised," said Megan quickly. "I thought you would have something more interesting to do at Christmas."

Giles smiled and put an arm lightly around Megan's shoulders. "You're a funny little thing, Megan Jones," he said. "I never know what is going on inside that pretty head of yours."

At his touch Megan stiffened; every fibre of her being prickled with awareness of him. "I just thought you would be spending Christmas with exciting, glamorous friends in London, or with your wife," she said at last, making herself mention the word wife.

"My wife is dead, and we usually spend Christmas with her sister Fiona," he said casually, "but not this year — the first time for ten years. That is why Joanna is so excited at the prospect of a real English Christmas."

"Oh," was all Megan was able to manage, unable to think of anything else intelligent to say. She was dying to ask when his wife had died, and why did he always spend Christmas with her sister. The unspoken questions fell over one another in her mind, but her lips remained silent. Giles for his part didn't elaborate any further, and the opportunity to continue the conversation passed by as Richard and Joanna made their way back towards them.

"I think Joanna's getting tired now, sir," said Richard to Giles respectfully.

"Yes, I am, Dad," chimed in Joanna,

"and my leg is aching a bit."

"Can't say I'm exactly surprised," said her father with scant sympathy. "You should be grateful that all you've got is a leg in plaster and a bit of an ache."

"Oh I am! Don't be cross," said Joanna, hanging on to his arm.

Giles smiled down at his daughter, the tender look belying his words. He loves her a lot, though Megan, a dull ache in her heart as she wondered what else there was in his life that she didn't know about. Unhappily she thought about his sister-in-law. She instinctively felt that there was a strong link between Fiona and Giles, but why she should feel that way she didn't know. There was no logical reason, nothing he had said apart from the fact that they always spent their Christmases there; it was just an intuitive feeling she had.

After Giles Elliott and his daughter had left the party, Richard was so full of Joanna this and Joanna that, that Megan didn't have the heart to grumble at him. She did, however, have a word of warning for him. "I can see you've taken a fancy to Joanna," she began.

"You can say that again," said Richard dreamily. "Hasn't she got lovely hair — and those eyes!"

"She is only fifteen," Megan reminded him, "and the daughter of the Casualty Consultant. You are nearly twenty-one and that is a lot older."

"Rubbish," answered Richard indignantly. "She's nearly sixteen anyway."

Megan sighed. Who was she to be telling her brother who to fall for? She hadn't been very sensible herself, but thank goodness nobody knew how she felt. "I'd better ring Mum," was all she said, "to see if there is anything extra in the way of shopping she would like me to take down."

"Oh, Giles is going to do that," said Richard. "I gave him the telephone number; he said he wanted to speak Mum because he doesn't intend to come empty-handed."

"We don't need charity, Richard," interrupted Megan crossly. "If you invite people, you invite them — you don't ask them to bring things."

"For goodness' sake, Sis," Richard exploded, "you're so touchy lately! If I didn't know you better I'd say you were in love! I didn't ask him for anything, he insisted. He wants to take something for Mum."

Megan sighed again. Of course Richard was right, she could just imagine Giles Elliott insisting. But, brother Richard, you don't know how near you are to the truth, she thought ruefully. "Sorry," she said, "I am a bit snappy, I know. Put it down to old age!"

Richard laughed. "Old age?" he said, "You look ridiculously young, especially in those old jeans and without any make-up. When you and Joanna were standing by the side of Giles Elliott you could have been sisters."

It was Megan's turn to laugh now. "That's silly, Richard," she said. "But now you mention it, Giles Elliott told me the other day that I looked ridiculously young and I didn't take it as a compliment."

Richard laughed. "He probably meant it as one," he said. Then he added, "I wonder how old he is? He's probably aged prematurely because of all his problems."

"Aged prematurely?" said Megan. "Richard, just because the man has a few silver hairs at his temples does not mean to say he is in his dotage! Anyway, what problems?" she asked, trying not to sound too curious.

"Well, I don't know exactly," replied Richard, "but Joanna hinted that there were still problems between her mother's family and her father. Even though her mother has been dead for years and her aunt has lived in America for some time."

"Ten years at least," said Megan. "He told me they always spent Christmas there."

"Poor kid," said Richard with feeling.

"No wonder she feels lonely. She didn't tell me very much, just enough for me to know that she is unhappy. Giles Elliott and her mother were divorced, you know, before her death."

Megan suddenly remembered the phrase Giles had used during their conversation at dinner; *they say history always repeats itself* . . . He had suffered divorced parents and an unhappy childhood, and now it seemed that his own child was suffering.

Long after she had gone to bed that night, Megan lay and puzzled about the situation between Giles Elliott and his wife's family. She was sure that was the clue to Joanna's unhappiness, not just the fact that her mother was dead.

She turned restlessly. She had always imagined herself falling in love with a man who would love her and her alone, no one before or after. But in her heart of hearts she knew that was a romantic dream for teenagers only. The harsh reality of life was that there wasn't a choice. Someone came along and you fell in love, regardless of their suitability. There is only one thing to do, she thought finally. Just regard him as a friend and don't get emotionally involved! Although quite how she was going to manage that she didn't know, and spending Christmas with him wasn't going to make it any easier.

5

THE week preceding Christmas passed quickly. Two of the pupil nurses fell sick and as she was lucky enough to be off for the whole of Christmas Megan felt obliged to volunteer for extra duties. This meant working for three evenings until nine o'clock. The day before Christmas Eve was the day of the unit's Christmas party. It was to be held in Megan's office which had been emptied of its furniture for the occasion.

Juliet Moore and some of the other nurses from the evening and night duty rotas came in laden with home-made goodies. They soon transformed the office with Christmas decorations and balloons, and a huge bunch of mistletoe which Juliet hung in a strategic position over the doorway.

"No harm in hoping," she said with a wicked wink. "You never know, I might get kissed by Giles Elliott himself."

"Yes," sighed one of the pupil nurses new to the department, "he is absolutely gorgeous, isn't he? I've never seen anyone so dishy."

"He has been married, you know," remarked Megan in a voice as casual as she could muster, busying herself with pinning up paper-chains, "and he has a daughter nearly as old as you."

"Oh, I don't mind that," answered young Sally cheekily. "I've always had a penchant for older men." She struck what she imagined to be a sophisticated pose. "Do you think he'd fancy me?"

"Not if you look like that," piped up one of the other girls. "You look as if you've got a prolapsed disc, standing like that!" She ducked quickly as Sally threw a piece of holly at her and screeched with laughter.

"Girls!" remonstrated Megan. "I know it's Christmas and you are all feeling festive, but don't forget we still have patients coming in all the time."

"Not too many, I hope," giggled Sally, who had already had one glass of sherry. "What will they say if they are looked after by tipsy nurses!"

"There won't be any tipsy nurses," answered Megan firmly, "because if there are you'll have me to deal with." The firm tone of her voice left the juniors in no doubt of the consequences if they should overstep the limit.

The party got under way just before noon and soon the office was babbling with laughter and conversation. It had to be a prolonged lunch-time affair, for work carried on as usual, everyone popping in and out of the party as their job permitted. Luckily it was a slack day so most of the staff were able to enjoy the proceedings.

Giles Elliott came in and wedged his tall figure into a corner beside Megan, who was eating a sausage roll. "I thought sausage rolls made you scream!" he said, raising his eyebrows.

Megan blushed, remembering her remark of the evening of the revue party. "Well, these are rather special," she had to admit. "Juliet Moore made them and her cooking is absolutely mouth-watering."

"In that case I must sample one," he said, reaching out a long arm and removing a sausage roll from the plate Sally was carrying past.

Juliet Moore battled her way across the room and joined them. "Do you like them?" she asked, watching him bite into it.

"Delicious," was his verdict. "Although I knew it would be. If Megan gives a sausage roll her seal of approval it must be good."

Juliet laughed. "Thank you, that's very high praise indeed." She sipped her glass of wine. "Are you going home for Christmas, Megan?" she asked.

"Yes," said Megan, wondering what on earth they would all say if they knew Giles Elliott was going to spend it with her. "What are you doing?"

"Oh, I'm home for Christmas Day," answered Juliet, "then I'm working Boxing Day and the day after. The money will come in useful for the holiday we are planning next year."

"Are you planning to go somewhere exotic then?" asked Giles.

"Only Majorca," said Juliet, "but with a family it is pretty expensive, so we need all the extra pennies I can earn."

"I have some very good friends there," said Giles. "They run a delightful little restaurant near the beach at Puerto Soller. You must visit it; they make the best paella on the island."

Grateful for the change in conversation, Megan excused herself and moved across to where Johnny Cox was holding court to a bevy of giggling pupil nurses. She had been unsure of whether or not Giles would have wanted anyone in Casualty to know he was spending Christmas with her and her family. Anyway, *she* was quite certain that she preferred the rest of the staff to remain in ignorance, particularly the pupil nurses. Their minds only seem to run along the lines of the latest romance, real or imaginary, fuelled no doubt by the romantic stories they were always reading in all the women's magazines, she thought.

Johnny had picked off a sprig of mistletoe and was working his way along the line of giggling, blushing nurses, kissing them all one by one.

Megan sighed theatrically and crossed her arms. "You are incorrigible," she said severely. "Breaking all these young hearts!"

"It is they who are breaking mine," he said, dramatically clasping a hand to his chest. "With so many beautiful girls to choose from the strain is too much for me."

"You don't have to choose," said young Sally. "You can take us all to the Mess party tonight. That solves your problem."

Johnny's face fell and Megan laughed. "Serves you right," she said. "You've got your just desserts."

Johnny raised his eyebrows expressively. "Oh well, they say there's safety in numbers," he said with a laugh. "Are you coming tonight?"

"No, I've got to work, and then get ready to go down to Devon tomorrow. Anyway, I'm too old for the high jinks they get up to at the Mess party."

"Poor old lady," said Johnny, holding the mistletoe aloft. "Am I allowed to kiss such an antiquated thing?"

Out of the corner of her eye Megan could see Giles Elliott looking at them. Was it her imagination, or did his blue eyes have a steely glint of disapproval in them? Some inner devil prompted Megan to throw her arms around Johnny's neck and kiss him back with unusual enthusiasm.

"Well, now I know it really *is* Christmas," murmured a surprised Johnny. "I think that calls for an encore," and without further ado he proceeded to kiss her long and thoroughly. "Are you sure you won't change your mind and come to the party tonight?" he asked.

"Quite sure, Johnny," replied a slightly flustered Megan. She hadn't expected Johnny to react in the way he had, and hoped that he hadn't taken the kiss seriously — the very last thing she had expected or wanted.

She felt Giles Elliott's gaze cutting through the crowded room like a laser beam as she disentangled herself from Johnny's arms. "I'd better go back into Casualty and relieve someone else to come and have some fun," she muttered, making her escape through the doorway.

Straightening her cap, which, as ever, was askew on her shiny brown hair, she marched purposefully into Casualty. The first person she saw was one of the elderly auxiliaries, Thelma, sitting morosely at the desk, idly flipping over some old X-rays.

"Your turn to join the festivities," Megan said to her. I'll take over here."

"Really, Sister, are you sure?"

"Yes, of course, off you go," replied Megan. "I'll shout for help soon enough if it gets too busy."

The plump auxiliary scurried excitedly away. Christmas was the one time of year when all barriers were dropped in the hospital and all grades of staff fraternised with one another; it was something she looked forward to.

Megan watched her retreating figure, her fat legs encased in black stockings, the seams of which were invariably crooked. Today was no exception. She smiled slowly; good old Thelma, her sort were the salt of the earth. She worked hard for not much pay, never complained, not even when insults were heaped upon her by irate junior doctors, usually taking out on her their own inadequacies. She was always kind and understanding to patients and invariably ignored by the nursing hierarchy. Megan would have gladly had ten Thelmas for some of the new staff nurses she had had to tolerate over the years.

She wandered out to the reception area to talk to the girl at the desk, seeing that all was quiet. As she approached the desk the telephone rang and the girl picked it up. "Casualty, County General," she said. She listened for a few moments, then said briefly, "OK."

She turned to Megan, who by this time was standing beside her. "Badly injured baby, about ten months old, on the way in," she said.

"Just the baby?" asked Megan. "Nobody else? Is it a road accident?"

"No, it's not an RTA," replied the girl. "From what Ambulance Control *didn't* say I would think it's a battered baby, or to use the correct phraseology, a non-accidental injury."

Megan heaved a sigh. "These cases always make me feel sick," she said. "Let's hope it's not as bad as they say. I'd better go and warn Giles . . . Mr Elliott, that a case is on its way in." She left the reception area and walked quickly back towards the sound of the party, but before she reached the door of her office she met Giles Elliott in the corridor.

"I was wondering where you had got to," he said.

"There is a baby on its way in," said Megan, not wasting time. "Non-accidental injury by the sound of it."

Giles Elliott's face hardened. "Poor little beggar," he said under his breath.

The baby arrived a few minutes later in the ambulance accompanied by the parents, a weak-looking, undernourished girl of about nineteen and a young punky-looking father with a shock of pink hair. Their story was that the baby had fallen out of her cot, but neither Megan nor Giles Elliott could believe it. But protocol forbade them from expressing an opinion at that time, and in any case the most urgent thing was to try to do something for the baby.

Gently Megan undressed the unconcious little body, carefully noting the various bruises on the fragile arms and legs and in the small of the back just above the area of the kidneys.

"I would say this child has been consistently beaten," grated Giles to Megan through gritted teeth, "and now she appears to have been hit around the head."

Megan said nothing. In spite of her professional training she was having difficulty holding back the tears. The little mite in her arms was so weak and defenceless — how could anyone hit a baby like this, she thought.

Carefully and quickly Giles Elliott made his examination. Then he said to Megan grimly, "This child is in coma, her breathing is stertorous, the heart appears all right but the pupils are fixed and dilated and I can't get any reflex actions." He sighed and shoved his stethoscope in his pocket. "I'll ring for Mr Mason, the neurosurgeon, and ask him to come quickly. Perhaps he'll think it worth scanning her, although I wonder. I think perhaps things have gone too far already." He left the cubicle to make his way back to his office.

Megan called over Thelma, who had come hurrying back when she had heard there had been an admission. "You stay here with the baby. I'll have to speak to the parents, I suppose. Then they will just have to wait until Mr Elliott and Mr Mason can see them."

"Is it bad?" whispered Thelma anxiously.

Megan nodded grimly. "Yes, I think it's very bad." She swished the cubicle curtains tightly shut behind her and walked outside to the reception area where the mother and father were waiting.

"How long are you going to keep us waiting?" demanded the young father belligerently. "We've been here over half an hour already. We've got to get back — she's got to get me something to eat." He indicated his pathetic little wife.

Megan could see that the young

146

man was a bully; it was obvious from the frightened way his wife looked at him. Her panic-stricken eyes looked beseechingly at Megan. "Is my baby all right?" she asked in a quavering voice.

"Of course the baby's all right," interrupted her husband. "That damned kid makes enough noise all the time! You're making a lot of fuss about nothing, you should never have called the doctor."

"I'm afraid your daughter is very far from being all right," said Megan gently, looking at the young mother and ignoring the father.

"Here, what do you mean?" he interrupted, pushing himself between Megan and his young wife.

"I mean, Mr Smith," said Megan, her voice taking on a harder note, "that your child is seriously ill and you are going to have to wait here for some time. Mr Elliott has asked a consultant neurosurgeon to come down and give a second opinion. As soon as I have any news I will let you know. Now, if you will excuse me."

He stood looking at her with his mouth open, all his previous belligerence evaporating. Megan suddenly felt very sorry for them both. She knew from reading the scant notes on the baby that the father was unemployed and that they lived in a bedsit. Poor things, she thought: neither of you is equipped to deal with married life and a baby and this is the tragic result.

She made her way back to the cubicle where Thelma was keeping watch over the child. As soon as Megan entered she looked up anxiously. "I think the pulse is weaker," she said.

Swiftly Megan reached down and felt the tiny fluttering carotid pulse. Yes, it was weaker and uneven. "Get Mr Elliott," she said urgently, but even as she spoke the baby started fitting and then the heartbeat stopped. Automatically she pressed the cardiac arrest button by the side of the couch and within seconds the cardiac arrest team were there, quicker than usual as they were only a few yards away at the party in Megan's office.

Johnny Cox, the anaesthetist, was the first to arrive, for which Megan was thankful. He deftly slipped a small tube down the baby's throat and maintained the airway, something a less experienced anaesthetist wouldn't have been able to do so quickly. At the sound of the bell Giles Elliott had come running, and Mr Mason the neurosurgeon was with him. Megan worked feverishly with the rest of the team, desperately trying to resuscitate the tiny scrap of humanity lying on the couch, but after twenty minutes Giles Elliott told them to stop.

"It's obvious we've lost the battle," he said sadly. "Don't blame yourselves," he added as the whole team stood disconsolately in the cubicle. "I think the die was cast before this baby even reached hospital."

Megan felt hot tears pricking the back of her eyelids. I can't cry here, she thought desperately, not in front of everyone else. Slipping out of the cubicle she hurried along the corridor looking for somewhere quiet, somewhere where she could control the tide of wretchedness that threatened to engulf her. Juliet Moore came out of the party and saw her. "What's the matter?" she asked in alarm, seeing the stricken look on Megan's face.

"The baby has just . . . just died. We couldn't resuscitate it," gulped Megan, her brown eyes brimming with unshed tears. "I know it's silly, but I can't . . . " She stopped, tears choking her voice.

Juliet pushed open the door of Giles Elliott's office. "Go in there for a moment, no one is about," she said quietly. "Don't worry about anything. I'll go and sort things out and do whatever needs to be done." She pushed Megan into the office and closed the door behind her.

Megan walked across to the window and stood beside it, staring out with unseeing eyes. With a great effort she held back the tears, knowing that if she gave in to them they would come in a flood. So intent was she on controlling herself that she failed to hear the door of the office open quietly behind her.

"Megan?" Giles Elliott's voice startled her. "What are you doing here?"

"I . . . oh, I," she faltered keeping her back turned towards him.

Gently he placed a strong hand on her slim shoulder and firmly turned her to face him. Megan hung her head, tears trembling on the ends of her silken brown lashes.

"Is it the baby?" Giles' voice was strangely gentle.

Mutely Megan nodded her head. Then, before she could stop herself, the tears came spilling over in a great hiccuping sob. She felt herself pulled into strong encircling arms, comforting in their strength. Her cap gave up the unequal struggle and fell from her shiny hair as his lips murmured soft words of comfort and endearment against her dark brown curls. Megan clung unashamedly to him, the rough tweed of his jacket underneath his white coat prickling the soft skin of her cheeks. At length she raised a tear-stained face to his.

"What must you think of me?" she whispered faintly. "This is a very unprofessional way to behave. I'm sorry."

He smiled slowly; the blue of his eyes seemed darker and softer. "Don't be sorry for being human," he said. "I'm glad you care, although I'm sorry it has upset you so much."

Self-consciously Megan pushed him away and bent to retrieve her cap from the floor. "I'd better be going," she said with a faint tremble to her voice. "There must be plenty to do."

"Yes," he said, almost absent-mindedly watching her trying to pin her cap back on.

Now that she was out of his arms, away from him, the last few moments seemed unreal to Megan. Had he really been whispering endearments into her hair? Had he really been holding her close against the comforting warmth of his body? In spite of her unhappiness about the baby, Megan had felt a peace in his arms she didn't know existed before.

But now the easy intimacy had disappeared and she felt ill at ease. "I'll see you tomorrow then," she heard her voice stilted and embarrassed. "What time do you want me to be ready?"

"Oh, I would say about ten o'clock," he replied, "unless you would prefer it to be later. You will probably be tired after this evening's party."

Puzzled, Megan raised her eyebrows. "What party?" she asked. "I'm not going to any party."

"Johnny Cox told me he was taking you to the Mess party tonight," said Giles, sitting at his desk. He pulled a tray of notes towards him. "It will do you good to get out with some young people, enjoy yourself, take your

mind off today's unpleasant incident."
The tone of his voice dismissed her
and left Megan without an opportunity
to reply.

Blast Johnny Cox, she thought. He
really ought not to jump to conclusions,
and Giles Elliott had suddenly made
her feel as if she was about sixteen. Get
out with some young people indeed!
She wondered whether he was trying
to emphasise to her the difference in
their ages? Perhaps he sensed that she
liked him far more than she should.

Ah well, no use worrying about
it now, she thought as she dashed
into the ladies' cloakroom and quickly
tidied up her face. She didn't want
the whole department to know she'd
been howling. It wouldn't do her image
much good if the pupil nurses knew
she wasn't as cool and efficient as she
always seemed to be. On leaving the
cloakroom she bumped into Juliet.

"I've sorted everything out," said
Juliet. "The police have taken a
statement from Mr Elliott and the

parents of the baby have now left with the police to give their version of the incident."

"I'm sorry, Juliet," said Megan, "leaving you to cope with all the unpleasant things. I should have done all that."

"Nonsense," said Juliet, "don't worry about it. I'm glad I was here to help." She squeezed Megan's arm. "We none of us are as hardbitten as we like to think we are, and I think that's a good thing." She smiled reassuringly at Megan, who wondered whether she knew that Giles Elliott had come into the office and found her in tears.

After that Megan tried to keep herself as busy as possible for the rest of the afternoon, but the thought of the baby haunted her. She felt sad and angry; it had been such an unnecessary death. When Johnny Cox came up later, at about five o'clock, Megan was sitting at the desk in Casualty opposite the cubicles, bundling up notes ready for return to Medical Records.

"What time are you finishing here?" he asked.

"I'm off at nine," replied Megan. "And by the way, I've got a bone to pick with you. What do you mean by telling Giles Elliott I was going to the Mess party with you? You know I'm not."

"Well," said Johnny, "I didn't exactly tell him — in fact he suggested I take you. Seemed to think that perhaps you had taken that baby's death a bit hard."

Megan looked down quickly. "Yes, I did," she admitted quietly, "but I don't think going to a party would make me feel better. Still, I suppose it was a kind thought on his part."

Johnny laughed. "Yes, it was, wasn't it? I have an inkling he thinks I'm smitten with you. That's why he suggested it to me, although I was going to ask you again anyway."

"Thanks, but the answer is no," said Megan firmly, "and don't waste your time getting smitten with me;

156

I'm quite impervious to your charms — you should know that by now!"

Johnny sighed and perched himself on the edge of the desk. "You weren't the only one to feel upset about that baby," he said slowly. "There are times when as a doctor I feel damned useless, and that was one of them."

Impulsively Megan reached out and took his arm. "You did everything you could, everybody did."

"But it wasn't enough," answered Johnny in a strangely subdued voice. "It was not enough."

Megan looked at him. This was a Johnny she had never seen before, quite a different Johnny from the bright, breezy Canadian who never seemed to have a care in the world.

He took her hand. "Come to the party, just for a little while," he said persuasively.

Megan hesitated; what was there to lose? If she stayed in her flat she knew she would inevitably start to brood over the baby incident. "All right," she said slowly, "but I'm not going to stay late. I've got to get myself organised ready to go home to Devon in the morning."

Johnny swung his long legs round and jumped down from the desk. "Great," he said, beaming from ear to ear. "I'll pick you up at about a quarter to ten. By the way, wear something warm; the heating in that part of the building has broken down, so the Mess is freezing."

Megan had to laugh. "Trust you to leave the crucial bit of information until last," she said. "Now, off you go and let me get on. I'll see you outside the nurses' home."

Promptly at a quarter to ten she was waiting outside on the pavement, wrapped up to the ears in a huge woolly sweater, jeans and an anorak on top to keep out the biting north-easterly wind. Johnny came running down the hospital perimeter road, vigorously beating his arms round his chest to keep warm. "Race you to the Mess," he said as he ran past.

Megan joined him, having difficulty in keeping up with his long legs, and they arrived stumbling through the Mess door out of breath and pink in the face.

Susan North, who was already there, greeted them at the doorway shouting through the cacophony of noise, "Gracious, you two look healthy, positively rude with it."

"You should have joined us," said Johnny. "The keep-fit duo of the County General."

Susan laughed. "Since when have you been so keen on keep-fit?" she asked. "I thought the only exercise you got was raising your arm at the bar?"

"That is where you are wrong, my girl," said Johnny, wagging a finger at her. "There are many hidden facets about my character that have never been revealed. Remind me to tell you about them one day."

"I will," laughed Susan, leading the

way across to the bar which was festooned with balloons and streamers.

In spite of herself Megan soon began to enjoy the evening. Practically everyone in the hospital who was off duty appeared to be there. They played silly games and generally let their hair down.

"It's a good job this place is well away from patient areas," remarked Susan to Megan. "Do you remember the old Mess, right opposite Men's Surgical? There were always complaints about the noise then."

Megan laughed. "Yes, I do remember," she said, sipping her glass of punch.

"By the way," said Susan, "I still haven't managed to catch a glimpse of your new consultant, Giles Elliott, yet. How are things going? Are you getting on a little better with him now?"

"Oh, he's all right," said Megan non-committally, not sure how much she wanted to tell Susan.

"I gather that he has quite a

dishy young daughter, so he must be married," said Susan, eyeing Megan curiously. It was unlike her friend to clam up about anything, but Susan had the feeling that she was not going to get much information about Giles Elliott out of Megan.

"Yes, I've met his daughter," replied Megan and told Susan of the accident with the motor cycle and how she came to be involved.

Susan was intrigued. "You and Giles Elliott certainly seem to have a knack for being personally involved in accidents," she said. "You're not a casualty nurse for nothing! First *you* are his casualty, then his daughter."

Megan laughed. "It was the first time I've ever needed to go into Casualty as a patient — you make it sound as if I was always there."

"Ah," said Susan dreamily, "but it could be the beginning of a beautiful romance. Casualty nurse swept off her feet by Casualty consultant . . . " She threw out her arms dramatically.

"Romance begins after consultant revives Casualty nurse!"

Megan hooted with laughter. "Susan, you are ridiculous! Revived me, indeed! And as for having a romantic ending, forget it."

"Of course," said Susan, "I was forgetting there must be his wife. Where is she?"

"His wife is dead," replied Megan, "but before you go getting any more ridiculous ideas, let me tell you that he seems to be very involved with his wife's sister on the other side of the Atlantic."

"Oh," said Susan, her eyes growing bigger with curiosity. "Of course, there might not be anything in that, you know. He might be desperately searching for another mate."

"And he might not," said Megan practically. "He certainly doesn't give the impression that he is. Now, come on, let's go over and join Johnny."

"Honestly, Megan, I just don't understand how you can be so

disinterested," said Susan, following her. "If it was me I'd have found out everything there was to know about him by now."

"But I'm not you," pointed out Megan and adroitly changed the subject. However, although she successfully diverted Susan's interest it didn't help her much. She couldn't help wondering and thinking about Giles Elliott and his sister-in-law in Los Angeles. He had given no hint at all about his feelings, other than the fact that they kept in regular touch. She wondered whether or not he might tell her more about himself over the Christmas when they were at her home.

Just after midnight Megan decided she really must go. She was feeling tired anyway and it had been a long day with the extra duty she had done tacked on to her own. Johnny and Susan appeared to be getting along famously, dancing cheek to cheek to a smoochy number being played on the hi-fi.

Megan grabbed Jamie Green as he passed by, laden down with four pints of beer balanced precariously on a small tray. "Will you tell Johnny and Susan that I've gone on because I've got an early start tomorrow?" she asked.

Jamie glanced over in their direction. He grinned. "Sure," he said, "although somehow I don't think they are going to notice your absence!"

Megan laughed. "I think you're right," she agreed and made her departure. But as she walked down the hospital road back towards the nurses' home, she suddenly felt a tremendous sense of being alone. Almost everyone at the party had teamed up with someone of the opposite sex, and yet she had no one special in her life. True, she had lots of friends, but there was no one she could run to, no one in whose loving arms she could bury herself. She remembered Giles Elliott's strong, comforting arms that afternoon, holding her when she had been so upset.

Without warning her eyes filled with tears and she brushed a hand across them. How stupid to cry at a memory. Sensible young women like Sister Jones of the casualty department didn't do that!

6

AT a quarter to ten the telephone in Megan's room rang. It was Giles. "Are you up?" he asked.

"Of course I'm up," answered Megan. "I've been up for simply ages and I'm all ready."

"Good," he replied, "I'll be waiting outside the nurses' home in ten minutes. If we make an early start we can stop for a leisurely lunch on the way down. That is, if you would like to," he added.

"That would be lovely," said Megan, half of her wanting to have an intimate lunch with him in some little country pub, the other half warning her that the more time she spent alone with him the more likely she was to go on falling more and more hopelessly in love with him. You must remember he has another life that you know nothing of, outside the hospital, she told herself as she staggered into the lift laden down with Christmas packages.

Soon they were speeding through the countryside towards Devon. The threatened snow still hadn't come and only the light sprinkling of the previous fall remained, giving the countryside a frosted sugar-icing effect. It was a beautiful day, freezing cold and crisp. Brilliant sunshine streamed down from a clear blue sky.

"Enjoy the party last night?" asked Giles casually, not looking at Megan.

Startled she turned to look at him. His handsome profile was a mask of indifference, giving nothing away. "How did you know I went to the party?" she asked. "I didn't intend to go. I only made up my mind at the last minute."

"I rang your room and there was no answer, so I put two and two together," he answered.

"Well, just make sure your answer is four and not five," snapped Megan, feeling slightly annoyed.

"I'm usually pretty good at arithmetic," came the imperturbable reply. "What time did Johnny take you back? Not too late I hope."

"I'm sorry to have to tell you that your arithmetic is wrong," answered Megan, settling herself more comfortably into the deep seat in the front of his Mercedes. She left it at that. Damned if I'm going to satisfy his curiosity she thought — serves him right for jumping to conclusions!

Quickly Giles glanced at her, a cold glint of annoyance in his blue eyes. Megan stared back at him defiantly, challenging him to ask her what she meant. However, he didn't and a distinctly frosty silence reigned between them for the next few miles. The atmosphere inside this car isn't much different from that outside, thought Megan wryly, watching the fields and hedges speed by.

"You're quiet," remarked Giles after about twenty minutes.

"I'm thinking," answered Megan, which was true. She was thinking about the next two and a half days and how she was going to get through them. His presence was unnerving; the mere fact that she was sitting beside him sent delicious tingles through her, but at the same time warning bells were ringing in her head. Watch out, watch out, they said. He is a man you know very little about . . . She wondered whether an opportunity would present itself to ask him more about his family and sighed inwardly to herself when she thought about it. At least, she imagined the sigh had been an inward one, but evidently not, for Giles noticed.

"That's a sad sigh," he said. "Were you thinking about Johnny? I'm sorry you've been landed with me for Christmas. You'd be better off with Johnny, at least he's young and lively."

Megan stared at him in surprise. "I wasn't thinking of Johnny at all," she said, "and I didn't give a sad sigh. You are imagining things."

"Sorry," said Giles gently, "it's just that you've been so quiet I thought you were missing your young friends from the hospital."

Angrily Megan shifted in her seat so that she could look at him more easily. "I do wish you wouldn't keep on about me being young. I'm not a young girl, I'm a mature woman. And another thing," the words came tumbling out angrily as she got into her stride, "I'm not the slightest bit interested in Johnny Cox. He's a friend and always has been, but that is it, nothing more." She drew her breath in sharply. "So stop treating me as if I'm a recalcitrant teenager, and also stop behaving as if you are Old Father Time!" she added as an afterthought.

Giles threw back his dark head and roared with laughter. "All right, Megan, I'm sorry," he said. "I asked for that, didn't I? I'll treat you as a mature woman and you can treat me as a . . . "

"Friend," interrupted Megan swiftly, afraid of what he might have been going to say.

If Giles was surprised at her speedy interjection he gave no sign of it. He just laughed lightly and said, "It's a deal."

They were well into the patchwork of the Dorset countryside when he pulled up outside a quiet country pub. It was a long, low, thatched building and the first sight that greeted them as they walked in was a great roaring log fire in an inglenook fireplace at the far end of the ancient beamed room.

"That looks like a cosy place to sit for a pre-luncheon drink," said Giles, leading the way.

Megan agreed and sat on one of the polished shiny wooden seats beside the fireplace. A large, ancient golden labrador, grey at the muzzle and broad in the beam, lay stretched out in front of the fire.

"I'm afraid you'll have to push him out of the way, Miss," remarked the landlord, "if you want to get near the fire."

"I wouldn't dream of pushing him out of the way," said Megan. "He looks far too comfortable, and anyway it *is* his fireplace!"

The landlord laughed. "Reckon he thinks that too," he agreed.

Giles brought them both a small dry sherry and they sat together on the wooden seat looking at the menu. Megan tried hard not to notice the closeness of Giles, but try as she might she was very conscious of the pressure of his muscled thigh against hers. She wondered if her proximity had any effect on him, and stole a sideways glance at him from underneath her long brown lashes. No, she had to admit to herself, all he seemed to be interested in was studying the menu and deciding what he was going to have to eat.

Eventually he chose country fare for them. Homemade pâté, followed by squab pie and duchesse potatoes, with half a carafe of light rosé wine to go with the meal.

Giles raised his glass to Megan. "Here's to the next two days," he said.

Megan raised her glass to his and touched it. "Yes, here's to the next two days, to Christmas." Then she added the doubt that had been lurking at the back of her mind. "I only hope you won't find it all too boring. We never do anything very exciting."

Giles smiled at her, the intense blue of his eyes mellowing into a darker hue. "I'm not looking for excitement," he said, "I'm too old for that."

Megan laughed and raised a reproachful finger at him. "What did I say, Old Father Time!" she teased.

He gave a wry grin and sipped his wine. "Point taken," he said. "I'd forgotten our pact already — the old grey matter isn't working too well, evidently."

Impulsively Megan leaned forward and put her fingers on his lips as he mentioned the word "old' again. "You are *not* old," she said firmly. "In fact, at the risk of letting such praise go to your head, I'll tell you that one of our pupil nurses thinks you are absolutely dishy, to coin her phrase exactly!"

"You must tell me which one," murmured Giles gently, taking Megan's hand and pressing it against his lips in a gentle caress.

Megan's heart thumped against her rib cage, like an imprisoned bird trying to escape. The touch of his warm lips sent a golden glow throbbing throughout her being. For a few moments they seemed in a magic world of their own, encircled by the flickering light emitted from the dancing flames of the log fire.

The voice of the landlord broke the moment of enchantment. "Is everything to your liking?" he asked as he cleared some glasses from a nearby table.

"Yes, everything is to our liking," answered Giles, his blue eyes never leaving Megan's face. Megan lowered her eyes, her long lashes fluttering in charming confusion against her delicate cheekbones. Yes, everything was to her liking too. Suddenly she viewed the prospect of the next two days with something approaching elation.

The meal was delicious, the pâté just right, not too rich, and the squab pie was, as Giles said, "Something out of this world."

"Although I'm from the West Country, do you know I've never eaten it before," confessed Megan as she tucked into the delicate fluffed pastry filled with tender pieces of pigeon and apple, subtley flavoured with spice.

"Shame on you," said Giles with mock severity. "I would have thought you'd have known how to make it."

"I'm afraid I've not done much cooking," admitted Megan shame-facedly. "My mother is such a good cook and she always encouraged me to study and not to waste time in the kitchen."

"Do you think it is a waste of time

for a woman to cook?" asked Giles, raising his eyebrows.

"Oh no, I certainly don't," answered Megan vehemently. "I'd love to have more time to cook, and to have a kitchen of my own, but," she shrugged her shoulders, "things just haven't worked out that way."

"You'll get married to some handsome young man soon, I'm sure," said Giles smoothly, "and have the kitchen of your dreams."

Megan chose not to answer but took a sip of her wine instead. "I suppose we mustn't take too long over lunch," she said, looking at her watch. "It gets dark awfully early now, and Mother will worry if we are late."

"You are right, of course," answered Giles. "The last thing we want is for your mother to be worrying on Christmas Eve, of all nights."

By the time they arrived at the tiny hamlet set in the rolling Devon countryside of the Exe estuary it was well and truly dark. Even so, Megan's heart leaped joyfully as each familiar landmark loomed up in the car's headlights out of the darkness; it seemed such a long time since she had been home.

Her mother, Richard and Joanna hobbling in her plaster cast, crowded into the hall to greet them. The old house looked festive, bedecked everywhere with dark green holly encrusted with glistening red berries. A huge Christmas tree stood in one corner of the lounge, decorated with traditional corn dollies and white stars.

Megan exclaimed at the tree. "It's lovely, Mum. I've never seen the tree decorated so beautifully before!"

"You've got Joanna to thank for that," answered her mother, taking the Christmas packages from Megan and piling them up beneath the branches. "She insisted on buying all those lovely decorations and spent hours tying them on."

"After she had nearly killed me by dragging me around the plantation near

Dartmoor! I think we inspected every tree on the place before she eventually chose this one!" The affectionate look Richard gave Joanna belied the grumbling tone of his voice.

"I don't know what you are grumbling about," laughed Joanna. "I'm the one in plaster, not you."

"It doesn't seem to have affected you at all," remarked Giles.

Joanna kissed her father warmly on the cheek. "No, it hasn't. I'm absolutely fine, Dad, and I just know this is going to be the best Christmas we've had for years and years." She tugged at his arm. "Come on, I'll show you to your room, if that's all right, Mrs Jones," she added.

Megan's mother laughed. "Of course it is, off you go — and for goodness' sake be careful of that leg of yours as you go upstairs."

Later, as she sat on the bed in Megan's room watching her unpack, she said, "How long have you known Giles Elliott and his daughter?"

"Only since he came to the County General as the new consultant," said Megan, carefully folding the clothes she was putting away in the chest of drawers.

"You seem to have got very friendly with him in a short space of time," observed her mother.

"Not *that* friendly, Mother," said Megan sharply. The last thing she wanted was her mother jumping to conclusions, especially as she was so uncertain about Giles' feelings for her. "Richard seems to have taken a fancy to young Joanna, so you can blame him for landing them on us for this Christmas."

"I'm not blaming anyone," said her mother quietly, watching Megan thoughtfully. "I'm very pleased they came. Joanna seems rather lonely and I gather she doesn't see a lot of her father as she is away at school."

"Well, you know more than I do then," said Megan, slamming the drawer shut with a finality that matched

179

the tone of her voice. "Giles Elliott and I are really only casual acquaintances through our work, and I haven't had the opportunity, nor would I dream," she added firmly, "of asking him any personal questions."

"Quite right," said her mother, taking the hint and answering equally firmly. "Now, come downstairs and we'll have a cold supper. I've some lovely honey roast ham and some home-made pickles. I take it you will be going to midnight mass as usual?"

"Yes," said Megan, linking her arm through her mother's, regretting that she had snapped her head off. "You know, I always love the Christmas Eve service. Are you coming?"

"Well, if you don't mind, dear, I think I'll stay at home. My rheumatism has been playing me up lately, and you know how cold that old church is." She squeezed Megan's arm. "I'll watch the TV in the warm and have some mulled wine and hot mince pies ready for you all when you come in."

Megan laughed. "Mmmm, mulled wine and hot mince pies, that sounds delicious. Very well then, I shall allow you to miss the service this year!"

In the event only Megan and Giles went to the midnight service. Joanna had said her toes would freeze and drop off from out of her plaster, and Megan had to admit she had a point there. So Richard elected to stay at home and keep his mother and Joanna company.

Giles and Megan walked to the little ancient grey stone church set amid dark, rustling yew trees at the far end of the village near to the sea. Megan had always loved it there because of the ever-present whispering of the trees and the distant sound of the sea on the rocks. No matter how still the air, summer or winter, the rippling sighs of the trees and the muffled roar of the sea could always be heard. As a child she had always fancied they were the voices of the village people from centuries past, friendly voices, comforting, a constant link with the past.

As they walked up the moss-grown path towards the warm light streaming from the open church doorway, the frosty ground crackled beneath their feet and Megan wondered what on earth Giles would say if he knew her fanciful thoughts.

The small church was crowded with village folk, all of whom greeted Megan with friendly nods and waves before the simple service began. The simplicity of the service was matched by the simplicity of the decor of the church. Just a simple crib lit by candles in the north transept, the church dimly lit by old-fashioned gas lamps hanging in cast iron chandeliers from the stone-vaulted ceiling. The parish council had been threatening to put in electricity for years, but it had been fiercely resisted by the villagers. Megan was glad. It wouldn't seem the same with electricity, even though it did mean everyone had to carry a torch in order to read the words from the hymn book.

The service finished with the bell-ringers pulling their ropes with enthusiasm and the old bells singing out loud and clear, announcing the start of another Christmas Day to the surrounding silent countryside. Megan and Giles walked back slowly after wishing everyone outside the church a happy Christmas.

"That was lovely," said Giles quietly, taking her arm and tucking it through his. "I really feel that Christmas has begun."

"So do I," answered Megan. "I never do, you know, not until I've been to the Christmas service, particularly the Christmas Eve service here. Perhaps it's because the church is so old. Seven hundred years," she said slowly. "It's nice to think that for seven hundred years people have been walking where we are walking now, coming back from church on Christmas Eve."

"Yes," said Giles softly, "I wonder

what all those other people were like?"

Megan smiled in the darkness. Suddenly she felt that Giles wouldn't laugh at her fanciful thoughts about the whispering voices. Perhaps one day she would tell him. "Not so very different from us, I shouldn't wonder," she said.

Giles stopped for a moment. "You're smiling," he said. "I can tell by your voice." Then he sighed. "There's a lot I don't know about you, Megan Jones."

"There's a lot I don't know about you, Giles Elliott," rejoined Megan. "Now come on, race you back to the house. Mother will be furious if her mulled wine is spoiled."

They ran laughing through the cold night air, and as they reached the house the first large flakes of snow began to fall softly, silently, down from the dark sky.

Megan lifted up her hands and caught some snowflakes on her fur mittens. "It's going to be a white Christmas after all," she said delightedly, holding the snowflakes on her mittens up to the light in the porch. "Look at them," she said to Giles. "See how they glisten!"

"Yes," he replied, looking at the snowflakes shining in her dark hair. "I had a feeling it was going to be a perfect Christmas. Happy Christmas, Megan." Gently he leaned forward and brushed his warm lips against hers with infinite tenderness.

"Happy Christmas, Giles," whispered Megan, her eyes shining like stars.

Long afterwards as she lay in bed reliving that tender moment, Megan wondered whether he would have kissed her again if they had not been interrupted. Restlessly she turned in bed. No point in surmising on what might have happened, she reflected. It didn't, so just leave it at that, my girl. In fact just after that kiss the door had burst open and Joanna and Richard had dragged them in.

"We heard your footsteps running up the gravel path," said Joanna, and then she too had exclaimed in delight at the sight of the huge snowflakes which by now were falling thickly and furiously to the ground. "Perhaps we'll be snowed up, cut off from the outside world for days and days," she said to her father.

Giles had laughed gently. "There's no use in us indulging in wishful thinking," he said. "Modern snow-ploughs are very efficient and Megan is due back on duty the day after Boxing Day, and we are due in London."

Megan looked at him curiously for a moment as his eyes met hers over Joanna's head. Did he really wish that he could stay longer? There had been no time for her to reflect however, as her mother had come in from the kitchen with a huge jug of steaming mulled wine and a great oval dish of piping hot mince pies.

They settled round the brick fire-place, where the logs were burning brightly, for Richard had just replenished them, and Megan found herself sitting beside Giles. He had her father's old chair by the fire and she curled up on the rug at his feet. Her mother sat in her own chair on the opposite side of the fire and Joanna and Richard dragged up the battered old sofa after turfing off the cat, who was very indignant and stalked out into the kitchen.

"You've upset Tiddles now for the whole Christmas," said Megan laughing as she watched the grey and white striped tail, bristling with indignation, disappear round the kitchen door.

"Don't you believe it," said Richard. "The only reason he's gone out into the kitchen is because he thinks he might find the turkey now that we are all in here."

They all laughed as Megan's mother said, "Well, he's going to be disappointed. I've firmly locked the larder door."

Giles reached forward and gently pulled Megan's shoulders back. "You don't look comfortable there," he said, "lean against me."

So she had, and had revelled in the sheer bliss of their physical contact. He had let his hand rest lightly on her shoulder, gently caressing her neck from time to time. Megan resisted the almost uncontrollable impulse to turn her head and kiss his hand. She wanted to so much, it seemed such a natural thing to do. The mulled wine went to her head, inducing a languorous state of well-being and before long her head was nodding against Giles' knee, her eyelids drooping with tiredness.

"I think it's time we all of us went to bed," observed Mrs Jones. "Otherwise I shall be too tired to cook the turkey tomorrow."

Megan stretched luxuriously in front of the now dying embers. "Today," she corrected her mother. "We are well and truly into Christmas Day." Giles clasped her hand and pulled her to her feet and for a moment their faces were very close together. His blue eyes were dark, unfathomable. Megan felt herself almost physically drawn closer to him by the power of his eyes and her gently curved lips parted in expectation.

"Shall we open our presents before we go to bed?" Joanna's voice cut through their invisible bond like a sword. "It *is* Christmas Day, after all."

Giles released Megan's hand abruptly and turned to his daughter. "No we certainly will not," he said firmly. "We'll open them when we get up in a few hours' time."

When everyone else had gone upstairs Megan waited with her mother, helping her to rake the ashes down to a safe level and putting the heavy old brass fireguard in front of the fire. Then together they checked the locks on the doors and windows, her mother having one last look at the huge turkey all ready on the dish, filled with stuffing and covered with rashers of bacon ready for the oven.

"Just to make sure Tiddles hasn't managed to get at it," said Mrs Jones.

Megan laughed. "And what would

you do if he had?" she asked.

"Cover the piece he had chewed with some extra rashers of bacon," answered her mother. "It wouldn't be the first time I've had to do that."

"Mum, you've never told me that before!" said Megan, her eyes wide in surprise.

"There are a great many things I haven't told you," said her mother with a twinkle in her eye. "Goodnight, dear. Sleep tight, don't wake until morning light."

Megan kissed her goodnight, smiling at those familiar words, her mind leaping back through time to all the past Christmases she had heard those selfsame words. Impulsively she flung her arms around her mother. "Goodnight, Mum, God bless. It's so good to be home."

"It's good to have you home and it's lovely to have a house full of people. I'm so glad Richard invited Giles and Joanna down."

"So am I," Megan heard herself

admitting, not noticing her mother's knowing smile. So that was how she came to be lying snugly tucked up in her warm bed, reflecting happily on everything Giles Elliott had said and done since the moment he had picked her up outside the nurses' home.

7

CHRISTMAS morning dawned and the bright light filtering through the heavy curtains in Megan's room told her that there must have been a substantial fall of snow during the night. Excitedly she scrambled out of bed and flung back the curtains. Yes, everything was covered in a fluffy white blanket, the clouds had rolled away with the darkness and bright sparkling sunlight reflected from a million snow crystals.

They breakfasted all together in the kitchen, just coffee and rolls while the presents were brought in from under the tree and distributed. Mrs Jones had got up earlier than everyone else and had already put the turkey in the oven, so a delicious smell of roasting meat and bacon wafted through the warm kitchen, permeating the entire house.

Getting presents for her mother and Richard had been easy. Richard always needed clothes — he never spent his grant on frivolities, such as he considered clothes to be — and her mother liked Worth perfume, which was a luxury she couldn't afford to indulge in. However, when it had come to getting something small for Giles and Joanna she had been at a loss. In the end she had bought Joanna a very pretty pair of pink fluffy bedsocks. Joanna was delighted with them and put one on her plastered foot immediately.

"Does the colour suit me?" she asked, waving her leg about.

"You'd better put the other one on your head," answered her father laughing, "otherwise you'll wear one out and be left with an odd one." Playfully Joanna flipped him round the ears with the remaining pink sock.

For Giles, Megan had eventually bought a tie from the hospital shop. They had recently started selling ties with the motif of the County General embroidered on them, the outline of a rose in a castle.

"It's not very exciting," said Megan as Giles unwrapped his present, "but I had no idea of your likes or dislikes."

"It's lovely!" he said. "Now I feel that I really belong to the County General." He examined it. "What an unusual motif."

"Oh, it's some ancient design from the knights of William the Conqueror — some of them settled in the area after they had conquered the English," said Richard. "It tells you all about it in the town guide, but I'm afraid I have forgotten all the details."

"Anyway, Richard, we don't want a history lesson now," interrupted Joanna. "What have you got Megan, Dad?"

"Oh yes," said Giles, putting his hand into his pocket and bringing out a small box. "I'd almost forgotten." He handed Megan a very small parcel indeed.

Even before she opened it Megan knew from the shape and size of the box that it must be a ring. Deliberately she didn't look at her mother, who she knew had fallen for Giles hook, line and sinker and was hoping against hope that her daughter had too. Megan hoped her mother wouldn't read too much significance into the fact that he was giving her a ring, but she was totally unprepared for the exquisite beauty of the tiny jewel that winked up at her from the box. It was in the shape of a tiny butterfly, delicately wrought in a gold filigree, with vivid blue stones for the wings.

"It's beautiful," breathed Megan, "but you shouldn't have given me something so expensive — I've only given you a tie!"

"It's the thought that counts," said Giles, taking the ring from its box. "That's what I've always been taught. I hope you like sapphires; you don't consider them unlucky or anything do you?"

"Unlucky!" echoed Megan. "On the contrary, I consider myself very lucky indeed to be given such a lovely piece of jewellery."

Giles took her right hand and slipped the ring on the fourth finger; it was a perfect fit. "That's good guesswork on my part," he said. "I had to estimate the size of your fingers, not an easy task."

Megan held out her hand to her mother and the tiny jewelled butterfly sparkled in the light. "I don't know what to say," she murmured.

"You don't have to say anything," he answered, "it's a thank-you for putting up with me this Christmas!" As he spoke it seemed to Megan that his eyes held a question in them.

For Megan's mother he had chosen a pair of beautifully hand-sewn sheepskin slippers and gloves. "I'm afraid I cheated a bit here," he said as she tried them on. "Richard told me what size to get."

Mrs Jones walked around the kitchen

in her warm slippers, waving her fur-clad hands. Then she came to Giles and flung her arms around him. "I'm so glad you came," she said, "and it's not just because of the presents. It's absolutely lovely having an extended family, I wish it could always be like this."

"So do I," echoed Joanna, squeezing Richard's hand.

Briefly Megan looked at Giles, but his blue eyes gave nothing away as he rose from the table and started collecting the breakfast cups and saucers. "Let's get this lot cleared away," he said. "Otherwise we'll be sitting here chatting all day."

They all set to and soon everything was tidied and the vegetables prepared for lunch, the Christmas pudding simmering on the stove. It was just a question of waiting for everything to be cooked.

"Do you fancy a walk through the snow?" Giles asked Megan. "I'm not going to suggest Joanna comes with us — one leg in plaster is quite enough."

"Anyway, Richard and I are going to play Scrabble," said Joanna as Giles and Megan were putting on their coats.

Megan's mother hustled them out, making sure first that they were both warmly clad. "Don't fuss, Mum," protested Megan. "We are not going to the North Pole."

They crunched their way down the path, their boots making big tracks in the thick snow. "If we don't come back you'll know we've fallen in a snowdrift," shouted Megan as they turned the corner by the holly hedge.

"Or eloped!" she heard Joanna's voice shouting back.

Quickly Megan glanced at Giles, wondering if he had heard what his daughter had said, but he was a few steps ahead of her and appeared to have heard nothing.

Megan led the way down to the sea shore where the snow had melted a little and the marram grass of the sand dunes was poking through like a mass of hedgehog spines. The sea was calm, hardly a ripple on the water, and as the tide was out there was a large flat expanse of firm sand to walk on.

"You can walk from here right into Exmouth," said Megan. "I always loved this walk; the view across the estuary is beautiful. It's always the same, and yet it's never the same, the colours are always changing."

"Yes, it is lovely," agreed Giles. "So peaceful, no one here except us and the birds." He pulled Megan's arm through his and drew her closer to him. "I'm glad you liked the ring," he said.

"It's lovely," said Megan, feeling suddenly shy. "But I still think it is too expensive."

"I'm the best judge of that," he answered firmly as they strode along the sands.

Suddenly Megan saw the cormorant. It was drifting along in the ebb tide, plunging every now and then beneath the green water. "Look," she said excitedly, pulling at Giles' arm, "see the cormorant there? Look at him fishing."

Together they watched the cormorant patiently fishing until the tidal flow of water had carried him far away down the estuary and out towards the open sea. Megan turned to Giles, her eyes sparkling. "I have always loved watching them fish," she said. "As a small girl I . . . " But her words were lost as his mouth came down on hers in a firm and searching kiss. As he bent his head Megan caught her breath in a little sigh of expectation. The look in his eyes was one of mastery, and she found herself willingly submitting to his whim.

He had kissed her before, but never like this. His firm mouth moved over hers with an ardent persuasion, his arms tightened around her body, drawing her closer and closer to him, until Megan longed for him with a sensual passion that was painful. They were lost in a world of their own, fused together, moving in one accord, oblivious of the sand, sea and the wheeling gulls above their heads. Time stood still and Megan felt herself drowning, being sucked down into a whirling vortex of passion and desire. Urgently she pressed herself closer to him and eagerly her lips parted to allow his searching tongue to explore her mouth.

At last he drew back, his breathing coming in ragged gasps. Megan buried her face in his coat, afraid to show the wild emotions raging through her.

"You do something to me, Megan," he said in a voice thick with emotion. "I don't think I should be left alone with you. I can't answer for my actions."

Megan raised her head, her mouth curving in a tender, sensuous smile. "I'm not worried," she teased. "You can hardly make love to me here on the beach."

"I wouldn't count on it," he answered roughly. "Come on, let's get going." He started walking along the beach at a rapid speed, Megan almost having to run to keep up with him. She was puzzled and hurt. He had given her a ring, he had kissed her like a man possessed. She knew now without a shadow of doubt that he wanted her as much as she wanted him, so why had he suddenly changed?

They were brought to a sudden halt by a rush of water between the sand dunes. The tide had started to come in and any further progress along the beach was prevented by the surge of water into the deep inlet between the dunes.

Megan decided to take the bull by the horns while she still had the courage. "Why did you kiss me like that and then suddenly stop?" she demanded in a trembling voice.

"Because I couldn't help myself," he said slowly. He took her face between his hands and looked into her eyes long and tenderly. "I shouldn't have done that, I'm sorry," he said quietly. Then his face hardened. "I'm a man, and you are a very attractive woman — I succumb to attractive women very easily."

Megan's heart sank at his words. He was implying that there had been many women in his life. Almost as if she wanted to punish herself she had to ask, "Have there been many women in your life then?" She attempted to say the words lightly, but her voice trembled.

"More than I care to remember," came the harsh reply. "We'd better get back now, it must be nearly lunch-time."

"Yes," said Megan dully, trying to ignore the cold hard lump in her heart, "we don't want the turkey to be spoiled."

They walked back to the house, carefully keeping a foot of cold space between them. Although it might as well have been a million miles, thought Megan bitterly, her eyes stinging with unshed tears. She was too proud to let Giles see that he had hurt her deeply, and kept up a non-stop chatter of light-hearted nonsense. When they arrived at the house she made the excuse to change her clothes and darted quickly to her room. Once inside she flung herself on her big soft bed, ready to let the bitter tears fall unheeded, but she was strangely cold and dry inside and she couldn't cry, although the lump in her throat threatened to choke her.

At last she got up and carefully put on some more make-up. It would never do to go down to lunch looking anything less than radiant. As she was about to leave the room the sunlight shining through the window caught the ring and sparkled on the tiny blue butterfly. Impulsively Megan took it off and put it away in its box. She didn't want to wear his ring! Damn him, she wished he could go now so that she wouldn't have to sit opposite him for lunch and supper, and lunch again tomorrow. Damn, damn the man. Why had he kissed her like that? He had made her believe she was something special to him and then he had cruelly told her he was susceptible to pretty women. Although she had to admit he had tried to be kind when he had told her, the hurt was just as bad.

Defiantly she tilted her head as she descended the wooden staircase. Well, I'm not susceptible to you, she thought angrily. Who are you kidding, came the nagging little voice at the back of her mind, you know darned well he makes you go weak at the knees!

Joanna noticed straight away as soon as they sat down at the table that Megan wasn't wearing her new ring. "Why have you taken it off?" she demanded with a young girl's frankness. "Don't you like it any more?"

"Of course I like it, silly," Megan forced a bright laugh and avoided looking at Giles. She was pretty sure he would probably know why she had taken it off. In a fit of, what should she call it? Pique? Yes, she supposed, that was the word. When he had given it to her a few short hours ago it had seemed the promise of golden things to come, but now it seemed almost visibly tarnished to her. How many other things had he given to attractive women, she wondered cynically. Her thoughts rambled on in unhappy confusion until suddenly she was aware that Joanna was still looking at her. "I think it is far too expensive to wear every day. I shall just wear it for special occasions," she said.

"If I like something I wear it all the time," said Joanna positively, "until it wears out."

"Rings don't wear out," said Giles, looking directly at Megan. His blue eyes pierced straight through her, seeming to sear into her very soul. "They last for ever."

"Yes," retorted Megan sharply, "isn't it unfortunate that people don't?" Perhaps luckily for her any further discussion was precluded by the arrival of Richard and her mother bringing in the steaming hot turkey, bowls of sprouts, carrots, potatoes and chestnut stuffing.

"I wonder this old table doesn't groan out loud under the weight of all this food," said Richard as he began to carve.

The traditional Christmas feast proceeded, everyone laughing and chattering, Megan laughing and chattering the loudest of all, but the food might just as well have been sawdust for all the taste it had in her mouth. And through it all she was careful not to address Giles directly. He seemed to avoid direct conversation with her too, and Megan wondered whether anyone other than her mother noticed. She knew she had, of course; it was impossible to keep any sort of situation from her mother's perceptive eye.

After lunch Megan helped her to wash up. Richard and Giles had both offered, but Mrs Jones had driven them fiercely out of the kitchen, saying, "You go and put your feet up, the pair of you. Just make sure you have a glass of port ready for Megan and I when we have finished."

They had protested a little, but it had been a half-hearted gesture, and then they beat a hasty retreat into the lounge to sit in front of the fire.

The kitchen was large and old-fashioned and had a huge double sink and drainers. Mrs Jones washed, her arms immersed in frothy bubbles up to the elbows and Megan rinsed and dried.

"Have you and Giles had an argument?" asked her mother, coming straight to the point.

"No," said Megan stiffly.

"Well?" asked her mother.

"Well what?" countered Megan.

"Well, what *has* happened between you two? Don't tell me nothing has, because when you went out this morning I could see that you were wrapped up in each other, but when you returned," she paused and looked at her daughter quizically, "well, that was a different matter."

"There was nothing different," answered Megan guardedly. "I think you have imagined something that was never there in the first place. I admit I like him," she added hastily, knowing that it would be impossible to fool her mother completely, "but he is a very attractive man, and lots of women like him. Women with a lot more to offer than I have. And anyway, I don't know much about him really."

"I think he is lonely," said her mother, sloshing the soap suds around in the sink. "He was divorced just before Joanna's mother died — of some rare liver complaint, I gather. Joanna was about four when she died, I know," she added as Megan raised her eyebrows at all this acquired knowledge, "because she told me. Her father has looked after her ever since and her aunt, who lives in America, has Joanna regularly to stay with her — something to do with her mother's will."

"That doesn't mean to say that he hasn't got some other special woman," said Megan practically. "After twelve years I should imagine he must have. He's quite a sexy sort of man, you know."

The moment she had let the words out she could have kicked herself. An almost triumphant look crossed her mother's face, and she knew she had let her feelings out of the bag.

"*Very sexy*," said Mrs Jones, "and of course one can't expect him to have led a celibate life — men aren't made that way. But I dare say the time will come when he will want to settle down with one woman again. If I was twenty years younger I'd go after him myself."

"Well you're not, thank God," said Megan sharply, "and for goodness' sake don't let him hear you talking such rubbish about settling down with one woman again. Even if he did, or ever does, it won't be with me! I don't want the man in my life to be shop-soiled and second-hand!"

Her mother gasped and stood with her soapy hands on her hips, oblivious of the water trickling down her apron. "Megan Jones, I never knew you were such a prig," she exclaimed. "Any man worth his salt has to have a bit of history behind him — you can't blame him for that."

"Since when have you become an expert on men?" Megan demanded angrily. "How many women had Dad practised on before you met him?" As the hurt look flashed across her mother's face Megan could have bitten out her tongue. "Oh, Mum, forgive me," she said, flinging her arms around her neck and bursting into tears. "I should never have said that."

Her mother held her tightly, stroking Megan's hair with her still damp hands. When Megan's sobs had subsided she held her gently away and looked into her face. "I should say sorry too," she said quietly. "I was prying into your affairs too deeply, and I know I drove you to that remark."

"It's no excuse though," sniffed Megan, wiping her eyes on the corner of her striped apron. "I suppose I might as well confess to you, though, that I do love that damned man. At least I think I do, but I also know he's a womaniser. He has told me as much. To him I'm just one more reasonably attractive woman, and he has a weakness for them, he told me so himself. That's probably why his wife divorced him." She sniffed again and her mother proffered her a large white handkerchief from the pocket of her apron. Gratefully Megan accepted it and blew her nose.

Mrs Jones returned to the washing-up. "I won't ask any more questions," she said, "but just remember the old saying, don't judge a book by its cover."

Megan smiled as she too returned to the dishes. Trust her mother, she always looked for good in everyone, and the strange thing was that she always seemed to find it. Wishing she could be as charitable as that, Megan continued with the pots and pans.

After lunch they all snoozed in front of the fire. Megan had explained her red eyes by saying there must be something in the kitchen that she was allergic to. Later on Joanna and Richard got out the cards and insisted that everyone play Snap. The game progressed fast and furiously, and Megan's unhappiness began to evaporate a little as she entered into the noisy spirit of the game. She was quick off the mark to shout and snatch the cards from the centre of the table when she had turned up a matching card — so much so that Richard accused her of cheating.

"Stop arguing, you two," remonstrated their mother. "Anyone would think you were children again!"

"Snap!" shouted Megan again, but this time simultaneously as Giles also called snap. Their hands moved over the centre of the table towards the pile of cards, coming down with only a split second between them. Megan felt her hand enveloped by Giles' large warm one and the warmth seemed to spread like liquid fire from his fingertips, running through her veins, setting her heart on fire. Against her will she felt her eyes irrevocably drawn to his and as she looked his blue eyes darkened with an enigmatic expression, locking her gaze to them.

For a split second the room seemed empty, just the two of them, and then Joanna's voice broke in. "You'll have to split the cards between you," she said. "Hurry up, we are waiting!"

As the cards were split by Richard, Megan mused over the strange effect Giles had on her, the effect of making her feel quite isolated with him, just the two of them. If only it could be like that for him too, she thought, dragging her attention reluctantly back to the game.

Their revelry was interrupted by the strident ringing of the telephone in the hall. Giles stood up immediately. "I think that will be for me," he said. "I took the liberty of telling Fiona to ring Joanna and me here at this time. I hope you don't mind."

Fiona ringing here from Los Angeles, thought Megan, totally unprepared for the odious pangs of jealousy that were overwhelming her. Don't be ridiculous she told herself sharply, it's not as if you mean anything to him anyway, and it is his family, even if she is his sister-in-law. But she couldn't help but notice the almost eager way he had stood up quickly when the telephone had rung. Yes, her instincts about Fiona were right, she was sure; she did mean something to him.

Joanna jumped up too to speak to her aunt and they could hear her telling her excitedly and in minute detail of every single thing they had done and eaten over the Christmas so far. When Giles spoke it was only for a few moments and his conversation consisted of monosyllabic replies. You're not giving much away thought Megan bitterly.

When they recommenced the card

game it soon became obvious that Giles' heart had gone out of it. Perhaps he's wishing he was with Fiona, thought Megan, torturing herself with visions of a beautiful woman with a face like a film star. She wondered whether Fiona was like her sister, Giles' dead ex-wife. She decided that if Joanna was anything to go by, her mother must have been a blonde as Joanna was so fair and Giles so dark. Perhaps that was the reason he had never remarried; perhaps that was the reason he was susceptible to attractive women; it was all a vain effort to blot out the memory of his ex-wife, a woman he was still in love with even though she no longer existed. Perhaps Fiona had now taken her place in his heart because of her similarity to her dead sister. Megan began to feel more and more miserable as her thoughts raced on chaotically. The obvious thing, she deduced, is that he probably never really wanted a divorce, but his wife died before they could be reconciled.

Common sense told her that all these

thoughts were totally irrational and that she had nothing concrete to go on, but nevertheless, having once got them into her head it was very difficult to dislodge them.

"Megan, are you playing or not?" demanded Richard. "That's the second call you've missed."

"Sorry," muttered Megan hastily, "I think the over-indulgence in food and wine is catching up on me, making me sluggish to say the least." Her voice sounded hollow in her ears.

"I agree," said Giles. "If it wasn't for the fact that it's dark, I would suggest that we all went out for a short walk."

"I've got an idea," said Richard, jumping up excitedly. "We've got that old sledge in the shed. Joanna could ride on that and we could take her for a brisk pull down the lane to the sea and back."

"But it's dark, as Giles has just said," pointed out his mother.

"So what?" said Richard as he made

his way through the door. "There won't be any traffic coming up our lane now, not on Christmas evening. A brisk three-quarters of an hour walk will do us all good and we can take torches with us. The exercise will make us ready for the Christmas cake and mince pies later on."

His mother groaned. "All you think about is food," she grumbled.

In no time at all Richard had got them organised and even Mrs Jones agreed to come, much to Megan's surprise. Joanna was seated in happy anticipation, clutching a lantern, on the sledge as they started off down the drive, Richard pulling the rope. Giles held on to Mrs Jones' arm as the snow was fairly deep and the wind had caused it to drift in places, but it was easy to see where they were going as the sky was clear and there was a bright moon.

"I think Joanna and I will have quite a difficult journey back tomorrow," Giles remarked as they trudged along in the snow. "That road along the Dorset coastline is quite exposed and I should imagine there could be drifting there."

Megan turned her head in sharp surprise. They were leaving tomorrow? She had been sure that the plan had been for Giles and Joanna to leave the day after Boxing Day.

Joanna obviously thought so too because she said, "Oh Dad, I thought we could stay all day tomorrow and go the day after?"

"I'm afraid not, young lady," came the brisk reply. "We've imposed on these good people long enough and we have to get the house in London ready for our New Year visitors."

Joanna pouted rebelliously. "I don't see why we can't stay tomorrow," she said, "then we can give Megan a lift back to the hospital."

"Megan will need to have her own car," Giles said dispassionately. Richard, of course, had driven down with Joanna in it.

"Richard can bring it back for her," said Joanna quickly, "after he has visited us in London."

"I see, the plot thickens," said Giles. Megan found it impossible from his tone of voice to know whether he was annoyed or not. She had forgotten that Richard was going to join them in London for the New Year celebrations as he had only mentioned it to her briefly.

She turned directly to Giles. "I don't want to be a nuisance to you," she said. "If dropping me off at the hospital is out of your way, Richard can always make his own way to London."

"Of course you wouldn't be a nuisance." His voice was tinged with a slight note of annoyance. "I have to go back to the hospital to pick up a few belongings anyway."

"Then that's settled," announced Joanna positively. "We'll leave the day after Boxing Day and give Megan a lift back."

"I was counting on you staying

tomorrow," affirmed Mrs Jones looking at Giles. "I'd planned to do a huge old-fashioned pot roast for lunch tomorrow."

Giles laughed. "It doesn't seem that I have a great deal of choice," he said. "How can I withstand all this pressure from the fairer sex?"

Easily, if you want to, thought Megan sourly. She knew well enough why Joanna wanted to stay — she wanted to be with Richard for as long as possible. She was also pretty certain in her own mind why Giles had wanted to go; he wanted to get away from her. Well, you needn't worry, thought Megan angrily, I'm not going to pester you and I'm certainly not going to be an addition to your long line of females!

It was in that more than slightly aggressive mood that she marched ahead of the group through the deep snow, and it was because her head was held high defiantly that she didn't notice the indentation in the snow. If she had, she would have known that it signified the presence of a deep hole, but as she didn't notice it she put her foot directly into it and immediately fell headlong.

She wasn't hurt, but her pride certainly was as she was hauled up unceremoniously, coughing and spitting out the lumps of icy snow that were in her mouth and that covered her from head to toe.

As he dragged her to her feet Giles remarked, "I seem to make a habit of picking you up."

"I don't need picking up," said Megan ungraciously. "I can manage very well on my own." She wrenched her arm from Giles' grasp and began to brush off the snow vigorously. He attempted to help but she twisted away out of his reach. "I can manage," she muttered in a low tone only audible to his ears.

"Perhaps we should leave tomorrow after all," he said, also in a low tone of voice meant only for her ears.

"Do as you please," hissed Megan,

"only don't just think of yourself, think of Joanna, Richard and my mother."

"I was thinking of you," came the reply.

Megan couldn't look up, even though she desperately wanted to. "Don't bother," she said coldly. "I don't care either way." It was a lie, but the words came tumbling out before she could stop them.

Richard drew the sledge up by the side of them. "You OK, Megan?" he asked.

"Yes," snapped Megan, feeling as if her nerves were being stretched to screaming point as Giles casually put an arm round her shoulders, sending shivering icicles of agitation prickling up and down her spine.

"Apart from her temper, she's all in one piece," he said. Megan rewarded him with a glower that would have quenched the spirit of any lesser man, but Giles only laughed. "You've got a blob of snow on the top of your head," he said infuriatingly as they

223

started walking again.

It seemed to Megan that as much as she was determined to have as little to do with Giles as possible, he on the other hand seemed equally determined to be as friendly as possible. Was it because Joanna had twisted his arm and he had to stay? Whatever the reason, Megan felt it wasn't good enough for him to blow hot and cold whenever he felt like it. She knew where she stood, and she was determined she was going to stand well back. You are dangerous, Giles Elliott, she said under her breath. A girl could get badly burned by you. You already have, taunted the little nagging voice from the deep recess of her mind, but Megan firmly quashed any such notion. She was an independent woman, she had never been twisted around any man's finger yet, and she was in no mood to be manipulated now!

In spite of everything Megan could not help but enjoy their moonlight walk in the snow which finished up with a snowball fight, started by Joanna of course, outside the house. When they were all too exhausted to throw another snowball they eventually went indoors, tired but glowing with good health, for a traditional Christmas tea of salmon and turkey sandwiches, sausage rolls, mince pies and Christmas cake. This put Megan in the awkward situation of having to sit with Giles by the fire while the others were busy in the kitchen. Determinedly she buried her nose in a book and made no attempt at conversation, but she found it impossible to concentrate. The printed words on the pages danced up and down before her eyes and Giles' face floated with maddening regularity across the pages, making her only too aware that he was sitting opposite her. He was watching her, she knew — she didn't have to look to know that, for an almost invisible thread linked them, making her aware of his every move.

It was Giles who eventually broke the uncomfortable silence. "I really *was* thinking of you," he said, "when I suggested we leave tomorrow. I feel that perhaps I've hurt your feelings."

"I can assure you that you haven't," said Megan stiffly. Pride forbade her to admit that he had done any such thing. "I can't think whatever gave you such a silly idea."

"I was thinking of that kiss on the beach," he said quietly.

"Really? said Megan in a nonchalant voice she could hardly believe was her own. "I would advise you not to give it another moment's thought. Since you made your position clear to me, I certainly haven't." She snapped her book shut with an air of finality that signalled the conversation was at an end. "Excuse me," she said, walking past him as he sat in her father's old armchair by the fireside, "I'm just going upstairs to freshen up before tea."

She didn't pause or look in Giles' direction but just kept going in what she hoped was a graceful and dignified exit, although her legs felt stiff and stilted and anything but graceful. As she mounted the stairs her heart felt as cold as the snow outside. I'm like the snow maiden in the fairy story she thought sadly — my heart has been turned to ice.

After that, Giles never mentioned the kiss or leaving early again. It seemed that he had taken a leaf out of her book, for he was a bright and cheerful companion with a ready joke for everyone — everyone, that was, except Megan. She wondered whether their armed truce, because that was what it felt like, was as evident to everyone else as it was to her, but to her relief nobody seemed to notice anything strange in their behaviour.

When at last Christmas Day had drawn to a close and she was alone in her bed, Megan turned her face into her pillow and wept. Everything seemed so hopeless. Why, oh why did she have to fall in love with a man who couldn't return her love?

8

THE thaw started on Boxing Day and Megan felt that it matched her mood perfectly. Everything was depressingly damp and dripping, the sky grey and overcast and bringing with it from the south-west a penetrating drizzle that soon turned the sparkling white of the countryside into a squelching mass of mud and slush.

"No drifts to worry about, Dad," remarked Joanna, for whom the sun was still shining as she was with Richard.

"No," replied Giles, "we should make good time back tomorrow if we leave early."

Can't wait to get rid of me, thought Megan, tempted to voice her thoughts, but determinedly biting back the malicious little devil inside her egging her on.

It wasn't until the next day when

they were just about to leave that Richard dropped his bombshell. At least, it was a bombshell as far as Megan was concerned.

He was kissing Joanna goodbye and shaking hands with Giles as they were about to pile into the car. "Goodbye," he said, "but not for long. I'm looking forward to meeting Fiona when I see you in London for the New Year. Joanna has told me quite a bit about her glamorous aunt."

At the mention of Fiona, Megan thought Giles looked slightly uncomfortable — or was it her imagination?

"It's a pity Megan can't come too," said Joanna, "and you too, Mrs Jones. Thank you again for having us for Christmas, it has been lovely."

Mrs Jones laughed. "London is not the place for me," she said. "I prefer Devon. And thank you for coming, it's been a pleasure. I hope I see you again in the not too distant future."

Megan ignored Joanna's remark about it being nice if she could go to London as well. Half of her would have liked to have gone, just to see what Giles' sister-in-law Fiona was like, but the other half wanted nothing to do with his other life — or his present life, come to that, she reminded herself.

Giles also chose to ignore Joanna's remark and just contented himself with thanking Megan's mother for her hospitality, kissing her warmly and shaking hands with Richard.

All the way back in the car Megan couldn't help thinking about the fact that Giles must have known all the time that Fiona was coming to London for the New Year, but he had never mentioned the fact. But then, she argued to herself reasonably, trying to be fair, why should he? He has no reason to tell you anything about his personal life; a kiss doesn't give you any rights, and anyway he said himself he shouldn't have kissed you like that. He's susceptible to attractive women, remember that. Megan sighed and leaned back in the seat. The only grain of comfort she could get out of the whole affair was that at least he thought of her as an attractive woman!

She thought of their journey down before Christmas. The physical closeness of his lean masculine body still did the same ridiculous things to her. She almost wished Joanna wasn't there with them, and then perhaps he would stop the car and draw her into his arms. She knew that if he did hold out his arms to her she would probably fall into them willingly, in spite of all the firm resolutions she had made about not getting involved! However, common sense told her that even if they were alone it was very unlikely that he would have made any move towards her. He regretted that impulsive kiss on the beach, he had admitted it to her. Turning slightly she studied his profile as he concentrated on driving through the heavy, lashing rain. His rugged masculinity was enough to turn any woman's head she decided, and unfortunately for her she was no exception.

When they finally drew up outside the nurses' home at the County General Megan didn't know whether she was glad or sorry. Just being near him gave her a sort of happiness, yet at the same time tore at her heart-strings in a manner that left her feeling confused and bewildered.

He helped her out with her luggage and loaded it into the lift for her. "You go and say goodbye to Joanna," he said gruffly. "I'll take your things up to your room. Give me your key."

Meekly Megan handed the key of her room to him as he commanded and turned back to the car to speak to Joanna. "Happy New Year, Joanna," she said, poking her head through the open car window. "I hope I see you sometime in the future."

Joanna impulsively flung her arms around Megan's neck, nearly throttling her. "Oh, I'd like to see you too, soon, soon, soon," she said with the exuberance of youth. "You're good for Dad, you know, I've never seen him so happy, not for simply ages. Although he was a bit off on Boxing Day. I don't know why."

Megan stared at her. She thought they had covered up very well and that no one had noticed things were strained between them on Boxing Day. "I thought he seemed the same all the time," she said, not knowing how to answer.

"You don't know my father very well yet," said Joanna. "I do, he likes you. I wish you'd get married."

Megan laughed shortly. "I don't think your father would like to hear you say that," she said, "and as for marrying me, I'm sorry to disappoint you, Joanna, but there is nothing further from his mind, or mine."

Joanna drew back and looked at Megan suspiciously. "Don't you like him?" she asked.

Megan took the opportunity to withdraw her head from the window as soon as Joanna had let go of her stranglehold on her. "Of course I like your father," she said, "but marriage is quite another thing."

"Wouldn't you want a step-daughter like me? Is that it?" Joanna's big blue eyes filled with sudden tears.

"It has nothing to do with you," Megan said firmly. Then she smiled and, reaching through the window, squeezed Joanna's hand. "And if I were to have a step-daughter, I'd choose one exactly like you. Now off you go to London! Have a lovely time with Aunt Fiona when she comes over, and leave your father to sort out his own romantic life."

Joanna leaned back in her seat with a long, mournful face. "I shan't have a lovely time with my aunt," she said. Then her face brightened. "But at least Richard will be there, so that will make things better."

She waved to Megan, who made her way into the tower block by now feeling more confused than ever. Whatever was going on, it was quite evident that Joanna was definitely not looking forward to the visit of her aunt, and yet she had seemed happy enough to talk to her on the telephone on Christmas Day. She wondered whether Joanna objected to Giles and Fiona being together. Perhaps she was jealous. Megan shrugged the thoughts from her mind. Whatever it was she was unlikely to know, so why waste time thinking about it?

She made her way up in the lift. There was no sign of Giles so she supposed he had dumped her bags in her room and was descending in the other lift. However, when she arrived he was still there, standing in the middle of her floor surrounded by her luggage, his presence dominating the tiny hospital room. Megan halted, startled to find him still there. Somehow his presence, unnerving for her at the best of times, was even more so in the confined space of her home.

Her pulse started racing erratically

as she stood with her hand nervously on the door handle. "Thank you for bringing up my bags," she said, hoping the falter in her voice didn't notice. "I'll wish you a happy New Year now, as I shall be working on that festive occasion." She tried to make a joke of it, but somehow her voice lacked brightness and it didn't sound in the least bit like a joke.

He didn't answer for a moment, just stood there silently in the middle of the room, looking at her with those all-seeing blue eyes of his. Suddenly Megan remembered Joanna's blue eyes, so similar to his but filled with tears a few moments before. "Joanna is looking forward to Richard joining you for the New Year," she said. "I hope you all have a wonderful time."

Giles suddenly looked grim and his face hardened. "I doubt it." he said. "Joanna doesn't want to go to America."

"What do you mean, go to America?" asked Megan. "I thought she lived with you? Why does she have to go to America?"

Giles sighed and suddenly Megan noticed the worry lines etched into his handsome face. Somehow they made him seem vulnerable, less arrogant and sure of himself. "There was a signed agreement which was that I should have Joanna until she reached the age of sixteen, which is in a few weeks' time, and then she is to go to the States to finish off her schooling until she is eighteen. Then she is free to choose wherever she wants to live. The trouble is, she doesn't want to go to America. She never did — and now she has met your brother," he sighed again, "she wants to go even less."

Spontaneously Megan put her hand on his arm. "I'm sorry if Richard has caused you extra worry," she said. "They are young, they think they are in love, but it will soon wear off and Joanna will probably have a good time in America." Even as she said it the words sounded false. She had seen for herself that Richard and Joanna had formed a deep attachment that wasn't going to be easily broken.

"You can't just switch off love," said Giles brusquely. "I'm only hoping that Fiona will be understanding."

"Well," said Megan, vainly searching for the right thing to say, "she must have been in love herself, so she will know what it feels like for Joanna."

"I doubt it," returned Giles grimly. Then he looked down at Megan's hand, which was still resting on his arm. Gently he removed it and raised her fingers to his warm lips. "Happy New Year," he said. "I'll be thinking of you working here."

He made no attempt to kiss her on the mouth, just closed the door quietly behind him and left. Megan stood still for a moment behind the closed door, then leaned against it and gently rubbed her hand against her cheek. For a split second when he had said, "You can't switch off love," she had thought he had been about to say something more, because the colour of his eyes had darkened as he had looked at her and she had felt sure he had wanted to kiss her. But he had not. His thoughts were preoccupied with his daughter and his sister-in-law, Fiona. Poor Joanna, thought Megan suddenly, her future had been decided for her years ago and now she was due to be shuttled off to the other side of the world with no say in the matter — although Megan guessed she would put up a pretty spirited fight to get what she wanted. She wondered whether Giles would support his daughter's wishes or whether he would feel bound by the promises he made so many years ago. No doubt Richard would tell her when she saw him next . . .

No use wasting time worrying about it now she thought practically. There was plenty to do before she went on duty the next morning.

In fact, once she was back in Casualty it seemed as if she had never been away and apart from the now rather tired-looking decorations that were still hanging up, it could easily have been that Christmas had never happened at all.

"Have a nice Christmas, dear?" asked Thelma.

"Yes thanks," said Megan, wondering what Thelma would say if she knew Giles Elliott had spent it with her. "Did you?"

"Not too bad, dear," said Thelma comfortably. "I was off on Christmas Day, then on duty for Boxing Day. Not that I minded, it meant my old man had to do the cooking and washing-up on Boxing Day, which makes a change. He doesn't do a thing unless he can help it."

Megan nodded sympathetically. She had seen Thelma's husband, a large man who looked a bit of a bully, and she knew from hospital gossip that he was. Apparently he believed that a woman's place was behind the sink, but he was not averse to spending Thelma's hard-earned wages, just so long as she did all the housework as well as working at the hospital. Megan often wondered why women put up with such a miserable life — but then, unless they had a marvellous job with a fantastic salary it was difficult for them to escape. At least, that was what everyone said, but Megan felt sure that she would have escaped by hook or by crook — and of course, she told herself, she would never have married such an unreasonable man in the first place. She would fall in love with a man who adored her! Some hope, her inner voice piped up.

Time for gossip or reflection was, however, shortlived, for the first admission of that morning was a child with severe upper airway obstruction. The child was three years old and had swallowed a peanut, so his parents said. As soon as she saw him Megan pressed the cardiac arrest button without waiting for the admitting senior house officer's opinion. The little boy was cyanosed and there was obviously a tracheal occlusion.

She was glad to see that Johnny Cox was the anaesthetist on the emergency team that day. He was so experienced that very few airway problems presented insurmountable difficulties for him.

"We need a tracheostomy to be performed here," said Johnny under his breath, "but I don't think we can afford to wait that long."

"Crycothyrotomy?" asked Megan quickly.

"Yes," said Johnny tersely, "we need to buy some time and it's the only way to do it."

Quickly the small boy was wheeled through into the small operating theatre at the side of Casualty. Megan sent Thelma to try to reassure the parents and she stayed with Johnny and the senior house officer while Johnny performed the dangerous and delicate procedure. There wasn't much time, for the child had become severely cyanosed and it was only a matter of moments before he would arrest. Megan watched the ECG monitor anxiously as they started.

With the patient supine on the table Johnny asked Megan to hold the child's head extended so that he could identify the cricothyroid membrane by palpation. This he did quickly, and then swiftly slid two large bore cannulae percutaneously through the cricothyroid membrane into the trachea.

"Oxygen," he said briefly.

The senior house officer quickly passed the suitable oxygen mask to deliver a high concentration of inspired oxygen over the cannulae.

Johnny stood up, beads of perspiration gathering on his brow. "God, that was a close shave," he said. "Let's get this kid up to ENT theatre now — fix it up with Theatre Sister, will you?" he nodded at Megan. "No arguments, tell her I'm on my way up with a desperately sick kid and we need the emergency theatre open and staffed and an ENT surgeon standing ready."

As they wheeled the boy away into the lift bay, Megan got swiftly on to the telephone. The ENT surgeon was already aware of the case as the other Casualty senior house officer had alerted him, and for once Sister Grover didn't say she didn't have enough staff and she didn't know how she was going to manage, or any of the other usual excuses she trotted out whenever there was a rush. It seemed that for a child even she was prepared to drop everything. Satisfied that all that could be done had been done, Megan turned her attention back to the anxious parents.

"I'll get Nurse here," indicating one of the pupil nurses, "to take you straight up to theatre now," she said. "I'm sorry we couldn't wait so that you could go up with him, but if Dr Cox hadn't done a crycothyrotomy your son would have been dead by now."

"What is that?" asked the mother, her face deathly pale with worry.

"Dr Cox has made a small hole

into the trachea through which your son is now breathing pure oxygen. It has bypassed the peanut which is obstructing his airway. I can tell you it's a very skilled procedure and we were very lucky that Dr Cox happened to be on duty today." Megan put her arms round the worried parents' shoulders. "Don't worry, I'm sure everything is going to be all right and he couldn't be in better hands. You go up to theatre now and the surgeon will speak to you. You will need to sign the consent forms."

"Yes, thank you, Sister," they muttered as the pupil nurse hurried them away. I only hope I wasn't over-optimistic, thought Megan, when I reassured them. I do hope everything is going to be all right. She knew from past experience that a seemingly simple thing like swallowing a peanut was potentially a tremendously hazardous situation. She sighed, for now she would be on tenterhooks until she knew whether or not that small boy came through the episode unscathed.

Luckily the rest of the morning was fairly uneventful. The cases consisted of minor burns and scalds, mostly two or three days old, sustained during the Christmas period, and the patients only realising they needed skilled treatment when the wound wouldn't heal. One broken leg and a broken collar bone from a riding accident made up the day's total.

It was nearly time for Megan to go off duty before she heard about the peanut boy. Johnny Cox rang down. "I meant to ring before," he said, "I know how you worry about kids. Thought I'd tell you our little laddy is going to be OK. He's got a tracheostomy of course, had quite a bit of laryngeal oedema from that wretched peanut, but once that has settled he should be as right as ninepence."

"Thanks for letting me know, Johnny," said Megan gratefully. "I know I should be more detached and not worry about my patients, but I can't help it."

Johnny laughed. "You stay the way you are," he said. "It's quite nice to have a Sister who is made of real flesh and blood for a change, and not some embittered old battle-axe."

"I shall probably end up like that," said Megan. "It's one of the hazards of the job."

"Nonsense," came Johnny's snort down the phone, "you'll be married with a load of kids soon if I'm not mistaken."

It was Megan's turn to laugh now. "I can't think what makes you think that, Johnny," she said, "and if I'm to have a load of kids, as you put it, I'd better get a move on. I'm no spring chicken you know."

"Well . . . er," Johnny hesitated for a moment, then he said, "I gather a certain consultant has been taking more than a passing interest in you lately, so it might be sooner than you think!"

Megan gasped in astonishment. "I don't know what you are talking about, Johnny Cox," she said indignantly.

"Don't listen to hospital gossip."

"Haven't heard any," came Johnny's laconic reply. "Just put two and two together and now you confirmed it for me!" He burst out laughing and put down the receiver his end.

Megan's cheeks were flaming as she replaced the phone. Damn Johnny Cox, he was too clever by far! He had tricked her into giving herself away. By telling him not to listen to hospital gossip she had implied that there was something to gossip about!

Once off duty and back in her small hospital flat she felt very restless. She almost wished she was back on duty — at least there was something to do then. She couldn't settle to read and she knew Susan had gone home as she had been on duty all over the Christmas, so she couldn't even go to see her and have a natter. She tried to ring her mother but there was an unobtainable noise on the line. Probably something wrong with the phone due to that dreadful weather, Megan thought. She rang the operator and reported the fault, then sat back and tried to concentrate on the book Richard had given her for Christmas. But it was no good, even with an almost superhuman effort on her part she couldn't keep her thoughts from continually straying back to Giles Elliott.

In the end she gave up trying and lay back in her easy chair, giving herself up to the painful luxury of remembering the way he had kissed her on the beach. No one had ever kissed her like that before. The memory was so vivid she knew that whatever happened to her in the years to come she would never forget that kiss.

The ringing of the telephone startled her out of her reminiscing. It was Johnny. "I'm off tonight," he announced, "and I've got the after-Christmas blues. There's a funny film on at the Odeon, do you fancy coming with me?"

"Oh yes, I'd love to," said Megan quickly. "I'm feeling a bit depressed myself. I always do when I come back from a visit home. A funny film is just what the doctor ordered."

Johnny laughed. "I'll pick you up in fifteen minutes. We'll see the film and buy some take-away chicken or something afterwards, if that's OK with you."

"Suits me fine," said Megan. "I'll meet you outside in about ten minutes."

Before she left her room she rang the switchboard, knowing her mother would probably ring as soon as the phone was back in order. It was one of the night girls she knew. "Oh, Eve," said Megan persuasively, "I know you are not supposed to do personal favours, but if my mother rings could you tell her that I've gone to the cinema with Johnny Cox? I did say I'd be in tonight but . . . "

" . . . But you've got a better offer," interrupted Eve.

Megan laughed. "Yes, you could say that," she agreed. "Goodnight, Eve, hope you are not too busy."

Eve groaned. "So do I, I'm on a

long shift tonight because of sickness. I've agreed to work right through until eight tomorrow morning — I must be mad."

"You'll get your reward, in heaven if not here!" Megan teased, smiling as she put down the phone. Then she hurried into the bathroom to get herself ready in time to meet Johnny.

The film was funny, very funny, and both Megan and Johnny laughed until their sides ached. It was only when they were walking briskly back, that Megan realised she had not even given Giles Elliott a thought for the last three and a half hours. There you are, it just shows, she told herself triumphantly. It wouldn't take much to make you forget him so you are not as besotted as you thought you were, my girl.

The idea that she was in command of her own emotions, or at least on the way to becoming in charge of them again, cheered her up even further. It was an unpleasantly wet, blowy evening, but Megan felt positively glowing with good cheer towards everyone. She hadn't been intending to invite Johnny in, although she knew he was hoping she would, so that he could sit down in comfort and eat his chicken and chips.

"I suppose your place is the tip it usually is?" she said.

Johnny groaned. "Yes," he replied, "I do try, Megan, but I'm just no good at housekeeping."

Megan looked at him with exasperation. "Honestly, Johnny, you are hopeless. You don't have to be good at housekeeping to keep a small hospital room tidy."

"Well, I've got all my research notes spread out," said Johnny defensively. "I can't move them until I've finished with them."

"If you tidied them up you might get your research written up and published," said Megan severely.

"Oh, do shut up," answered Johnny good-naturedly. "You are beginning to sound like my professor. Every time I see him he asks me if I have done my writing-up yet. It gets monotonous, I can tell you!"

Megan laughed. "Poor Johnny, nagged by everybody. All right, I won't nag you, I promise. Do you want to come up to my room and have your supper in comfort? I've got a bottle of red wine in the cupboard."

"Hell, it's taken you long enough to ask me," was Johnny's ungrateful reply, and he ducked swiftly to avoid being battered on the head by Megan with her parcel of chicken and chips.

On reaching her room Megan put up the small folding card table that served as a dining-table when she had visitors and set out the plates, knives and forks.

"My God, you're so civilised," was Johnny's comment. "I'd have eaten it straight out of the paper."

"Maybe you would, but I do prefer to be civilised," said Megan, "and so should you."

"I will be one day," answered the

unrepentant Johnny. "When I grow up."

Megan laughed. There was one thing about Johnny — it was impossible to stay annoyed with him. "I'm not so sure that you will ever do that," she said, handing him the bottle of wine to open. "That's a good wine, we ought to let it breathe really," she remarked as Johnny deftly uncorked the bottle.

"It can breathe in our stomachs," he replied as he poured out two glasses of the dark red wine. They sat opposite each other and Johnny raised his glass to Megan. "Here's to the New Year," he said. "Let's hope everything that happens is good."

"Amen to that," said Megan with feeling.

As they were eating their supper Johnny said casually, "What do you wish for the New Year, Megan? Would you like to get married?"

To her annoyance Megan felt herself blushing. Was he going to refer to Giles Elliott again? Or, worse still, was he going to propose to her? The thought stopped her dead in her tracks and she almost choked on a piece of chicken. Johnny, however, didn't wait for her to reply.

"I'm thinking of it," he announced.

"Thinking of what?" spluttered Megan.

"Getting married, of course," said Johnny, as if it was the most natural thing in the world for him to be contemplating.

Megan gulped and swallowed her piece of chicken. "I'm almost afraid to ask who the, er . . . " she hesitated, "lucky . . . girl is?"

Johnny laughed. "Don't worry, I know I don't come up to your high expectations of what a sensible and reliable man should be, but there is a girl who thinks quite highly of me." He frowned for a moment, then said, "At least, I think she does."

Megan remembered the party in the doctors' Mess before Christmas, and the dreamy way Johnny and Susan had been dancing together. "Susan North?" she asked.

Johnny raised his eyebrows in astonishment. "I knew you were clever," he said, "but I didn't know you were clairvoyant!"

Megan laughed. "I'm not, I just noticed you had become rather friendly at the Mess party before Christmas." She laughed again at Johnny's discomforted look. "I don't think you even remember that I was there," she said accusingly.

"Well, actually no," Johnny admitted. Then he leaned across the small table confidentially. "Do me a favour, Megan. Find out how I stand in Susan's estimation. I don't want to make a fool of myself if she's not interested."

"Johnny Cox," Megan erupted into laughter, "for all your bravado with the girls, you are a coward! No, I won't run your errands for you — you can do your own dirty work."

"Megan, *please*," he pleaded. "This time it's really important to me and I don't want to louse it up with my big mouth. Just prepare the ground a little for me, that's all I ask."

"Oh, all right," agreed Megan. "I'll see what I can do in the cause of true love!" She laughed again. "I never thought I'd start the New Year off playing Cupid!"

Johnny smiled sheepishly and poured Megan another glass of wine. "You're a good sort, Megan," he said. "Some man is going to be lucky one day."

"Humph," snorted Megan in reply.

When the chicken and chips were finished Megan carried the dirty dishes through the corridor into the kitchen she shared with four others, and fetched a piece of Camembert she had been saving. "This will go nicely with the rest of the wine," she announced, putting it on the table. "I'll just pop back to the kitchen and get some biscuits." The phone rang while she was in the kitchen. "Answer it for me, Johnny, will you?" she shouted. "It's probably my mother."

When she re-entered the room Johnny

handed her the phone with a strangely quizzical look on his face. "It's not your mother," he said.

"Hello," said Megan tentatively into the receiver, puzzling over Johnny's expression.

"Megan?" came a voice she knew so well. Even at long distance he sends shivers down my spine she thought inconsequentially.

"Oh, hello," she said, desperately trying to keep her voice light and non-committal. Partly for the benefit of Giles Elliott on the other end of the line and also partly for Johnny's benefit, for his expression had now changed to a smug, I-thought-so, sort of look.

"This is a surprise," she said. "What can I do for you?"

"Nothing," came the reply. "I just thought I'd ring and see how you were. I thought perhaps you might be lonely as most of your friends were still on leave." He laughed and it was a hard-sounding laugh. "But of course,

I should have known better, you young people are never alone for long. Have a good evening?"

"I've had an absolutely wonderful evening so far," said Megan, beginning to feel angry at his unspoken insinuations, "and I've no doubt that the rest of the evening will be just as good."

"I'm so glad to hear it," said Giles gruffly. "Young people always have a capacity for . . . "

"Oh, for goodness' sake don't keep on about that," snapped Megan, her patience evaporating completely. "Perhaps you should change from Casualty to Geriatrics!" It was terribly rude of her, she knew, but her blood just boiled when he kept referring to her as young!

There was a long silence on the other end of the line and for a moment Megan wondered whether he had put the phone down, but then he said, "I suppose I asked for that."

"You most certainly did," replied

Megan, then she deliberately changed the subject. "How is Joanna?"

"Fine, fretting for Richard to come down and join us, but otherwise fine."

"Has," Megan hesitated, then she took the plunge, "has your friend arrived from America yet?"

"My sister-in-law," corrected Giles. "Please don't forget that."

"Sorry," said Megan, "that's what I meant. Anyway, has she arrived?"

"Tomorrow," said Giles briefly. Then there was a silence.

Megan felt the tension between them even though they were so far apart, "I . . . er," she faltered awkwardly, "thank you for calling, I'd better go now as we are half-way through supper."

"Late supper," observed Giles, obviously expecting her to elaborate.

"Yes," said Megan, knowing he would jump to all the wrong conclusions but unable to say anything, particularly as Johnny was listening to every word. "Goodnight then, and thanks again for calling."

"Goodnight," replied Giles. His voice sounded distant and unfriendly and Megan had the distinct impression that he was regretting having phoned. The line clicked; he had put down the receiver.

Damn, damn, damn! Why had he phoned when Johnny was there? And to make matters even worse Johnny had answered for her.

"Thought you said it was just hospital gossip," he said casually, cutting himself a piece of cheese, as he watched Megan's face intently.

"Shut up," said Megan ungraciously, then she sighed. "Sorry, Johnny, I didn't mean to be rude."

"Perhaps I should do some ground-work for you in that direction," suggested Johnny.

"I would prefer you to mind your own business," answered Megan emphatically, "and leave some of the cheese for me!"

9

THE days up to the New Year passed quickly. Luckily for Megan, Casualty was frantically busy again, so she had little time to think of Giles Elliott, or of his mysterious sister-in-law, Fiona. Although when she was off duty her thoughts invariably returned to him — she couldn't help it. She wondered what decision had been reached regarding Joanna, but most of all she wondered about Fiona.

On New Year's Eve, just before midnight, Richard rang her from London. Megan was in the casualty department as she had volunteered to work the night. So many of the younger nurses had wanted to go to parties, and Megan hadn't any inclination for that. Anyway, she felt that in her present state of mind she would be much better working; that way at least she could push unbidden thoughts of Giles Elliott into the background of her mind.

"Happy New Year, Sis," shouted Richard.

"Happy New Year," echoed Joanna. Megan pictured them in her mind's eye, standing happily, arms twined around each other by the telephone in the elegant London house that belonged to Giles.

"Happy New Year," she said, trying to sound light-hearted.

"Are you busy?" asked Richard.

"Reasonably so," answered Megan. "We've had our share of road accidents, and no doubt we'll have some more when all the parties finish."

"Poor Megan," said Joanna, "having to work when everyone else is having a good time."

"Oh, I don't mind," said Megan. "When you work in a hospital you get used to it. When Richard qualifies, he will have to work at holiday times too, you know."

"Daddy isn't, thank goodness," said Joanna, but then she added, "but this is the first time he has had Christmas *and* New Year off for as long as I can remember."

"There you are then," said Megan. "So you see, I'm no exception." She paused a moment, then added casually, "How is your father?"

"Oh, all right I suppose," said Joanna. "He's been closeted in with Aunt Fiona most of the time since she arrived. Actually," she added in a confidential tone, "he hasn't been in a very good mood lately, in fact not since we came back from Devon."

Richard interrupted. "We can't stay on the phone for too long as Joanna's father will be footing the bill. Happy New Year again, Sis, and I'll see you soon."

"Take care," said Megan. "Give my regards to Giles, won't you and wish him a happy New Year for me."

"I thought perhaps you'd ring him yourself," said Richard.

"No, no, we are far too busy here," said Megan quickly. Much *too* quickly she knew. "You wish him a happy New Year for me. Goodbye to you both."

"Goodbye," came their two happy voices over the phone. Megan suddenly felt very miserable and alone indeed. She had successfully kept thoughts of Giles at bay for several days, but now with Richard's call the memories of him came back with painful clarity. Desperately she wished she could have been there with him, Joanna and Richard, and that wretched woman Fiona could have stayed on the other side of the Atlantic.

The long night dragged on interminably through to morning, and by the time she had finished her stint of duty she felt drained of everything except a deep feeling of unhappiness.

"Happy New Year," said Thelma brightly as she came on duty.

"What's happy about it?" asked Megan wearily. She certainly didn't feel happy and she didn't think Thelma had anything to feel particularly happy about.

"Sister," remonstrated Thelma good-naturedly, "I always think the next year must be better than the last — it's what keeps me going."

Megan smiled wanly. Trust Thelma to have a good, sensible philosophy she thought, feeling ashamed of herself. "You're right," she said. "I must think like that too. Think positive, as they say!"

"You'd be surprised at the difference it makes," said Thelma as she took off her cloak and hung it up. "I live my life in a permanent state of anticipation!" She laughed. "I'm usually disappointed, but never mind."

Megan felt even more ashamed. How stupid she had been, allowing herself to wallow in self-pity all night. She attempted to put on a brighter face. "Don't take any notice of me," she said. "I'm just tired, that's all. I'm not used to doing the night shift."

"What has happened to Sister Moore?" asked Thelma.

"She had last night off," said Megan. "I had all of Christmas, so she deserves the New Year." She paused at the door. "Happy New Year, Thelma, I hope that this year really does turn out to be a better one for you."

"So do I," answered Thelma with feeling.

Megan made her way back to her room thinking about Thelma's philosophy. There was no doubt about it, that was the way to look at life. I must try to do that, she thought as she climbed into bed and immediately fell soundly asleep, the sleep of exhaustion.

In the days following New Year Megan determinedly put Giles Elliott out of her mind, adopting the philosophy that the future would have to take care of itself. When Susan came back from her leave Megan cautiously sounded her out about Johnny Cox, as she had promised Johnny she would. To her surprise Susan was as enamoured of Johnny as he was of her, and equally unsure of his feelings. Susan, too, was afraid to show her true feelings in case she was rebuffed. Megan said nothing to Susan about Johnny; he's got to tell her himself, she thought, so she cornered him next time she saw him in the canteen.

"Have you seen Susan?" were his first words.

Megan smiled. "Yes, I've seen Susan," she answered, "and my advice to you is ask her out and tell her how you feel."

Johnny grinned from ear to ear. "You mean I've got a chance?" he asked incredulously.

"A very good one," said Megan briskly, "and from now on *you've* got to do all the work!"

Johnny reached across the table and squeezed Megan's hand. "Thanks, you're a real pal," he said. "I'll do the same for you one day." He bolted down the rest of his lunch. "I think I'll dash up to the orthopaedic ward before my theatre list this afternoon. Never know, I might just be able to have a quick word with her."

"Don't get her into trouble with Sister," warned Megan. "If Sister Warner is on today be careful, she has no sense of humour at all."

Johnny waved a hand airily as he got up from the table. "Don't worry, I'll use my irresistible charm on her!" All his old self-confidence had come bubbling back and he was on top of the world again.

Megan watched his retreating figure wistfully. Lucky Johnny and Susan. Why can't I have a love life, she thought mournfully. Why does Giles Elliott have to be free and yet somehow not free? Something or someone is there, I know, and I don't know what. Why couldn't I have met him before he was married — although he wouldn't have looked at me then, she reflected wryly, I would have been much too young and he wouldn't have had Joanna so Richard wouldn't have met her. If Richard hadn't met Joanna then Giles wouldn't have spent Christmas with them in Devon. She smiled ruefully. It was like a never-ending circle, full of ifs and buts! The only thing she bitterly regretted was that she had allowed herself to fall hopelessly in love with him, and that he obviously didn't love her. He was attracted, yes, but in love, no, she thought cynically. She gave herself a brisk mental shake; forget him, she instructed her wayward thoughts. If you can, came the nagging little voice which always popped up unbidden when she least wanted it to.

When she returned to Casualty after lunch there was a message scrawled for her on the notice board. *Sister Jones — please phone Mr Elliott* and it gave his London telephone number. Even the sight of his name scribbled on the noticeboard caused Megan's heart to lurch in an unruly manner. It was with trembling fingers that she dialled the number in her office. This is ridiculous, she told herself, no man is worth getting into such a state for.

Giles answered the telephone himself, almost as if he had been waiting for her to ring.

"Hello," said Megan, keeping her voice cool and efficient. "You left a message for me to ring."

"Yes, I did," said Giles in that soft voice which caused her heart to beat even faster. "How are you?"

"Fine," said Megan, wondering if that was the only reason he had rung. But why should he do that? He was returning to the casualty department in two days' time.

"I expect you are wondering why I rang," said Giles, voicing Megan's thoughts.

Megan hesitated. "Well, actually, yes I was," she confessed. "Is there something I can do for you?"

"Several things," answered Giles. "The first thing is, are you free on Thursday night?"

"Yes," said Megan, mystified, "I

hadn't planned to do anything."

"Good," said Giles. "Then would you please keep it free. I would like you to come out for a meal with Fiona, Joanna and me."

"You would?" asked Megan in surprise, not feeling particularly happy at the thought of having to sit through a meal with his sister-in-law. "Are you sure Fiona will want to meet me?"

"*I* want her to meet you," said Giles.

Megan began to feel a little irritated at the peculiar turn of events. "I can't think why — she and I can't possibly have anything in common."

"It's not for your benefit, or hers," answered Giles rather taciturnly, "nor mine either, but for Joanna." He paused, then sighed. "I'm sorry to draw you into what is really my family problem, but Joanna hasn't been easy to deal with. She has refused point blank to go to America and has told her aunt that she wants to finish her schooling in the south of England. I was thinking of sending her to your old school, as a boarder. It is relatively near the hospital, so she could come home at weekends if she wanted to. Joanna has persuaded her aunt that it is a good school and has cited you as a shining example of its products!" He laughed, but to Megan it sounded forced. "There, you should be flattered."

"I am, of course," answered Megan slowly, "but I left school a long time ago, although I have kept in touch and I know it hasn't changed that much."

"Yes, I know that because Richard told me," said Giles. "The other reason I'm bringing them both down is that Joanna is due to have an X-ray through her plaster, just to check that all is going well. I thought I could kill two birds with one stone."

"I see," said Megan. "Well, I don't really have much choice, do I?"

"Yes, of course you do," answered Giles quickly with a tinge of impatience.

"If you don't want to do it, just say no."

"I don't mind," said Megan, "as long as you remember that I shall only give my opinion on the school and not whether Joanna should go to America or stay in England."

"Don't worry, I wouldn't be so unthinking as to put you in that invidious position. I'll see you on Thursday then. Joanna has to attend the fracture clinic in the afternoon to see Mr Morgan. I'll let you know what time we'll pick you up in the evening."

"You needn't pick me up," said Megan quickly. "Just tell me where you are going and I'll get there."

"Without a car?" asked Giles. "Have you forgotten that Richard still has your car?"

Megan sighed. "For a moment, yes," she confessed. "I'll have to rely on you, I'm afraid. I've no alternative."

"I'm sorry," Giles' voice sounded clipped, "I know you prefer your independence. See you on Thursday."

Long after she had put down the phone Megan sat at her desk, drumming her fingers nervously, staring with unseeing eyes at the tattered Christmas decorations still hanging in her office. She felt a hard lump of apprehension at the thought of the meeting on Thursday. The idea of seeing Giles with Fiona she found almost unbearable, for she was a living link with his dead wife. Her thoughts returned to Giles once more. He had sounded so unfriendly on the telphone that she wondered whether he would have preferred Joanna to have gone to America — then quickly dismissed that as nonsense. If there was one thing she could be certain of it was the fact that he loved his daughter dearly and would do anything to make her happy. She wondered about Fiona again. What would she be like?

When Thursday arrived Megan found she had butterflies in her stomach from the moment she got up. Was it because of meeting Joanna's Aunt Fiona? Or was it because of seeing Giles again? She wasn't sure; perhaps it was a little of both she decided.

She saw Giles and Joanna briefly at the end of the corridor in the early afternoon, obviously on their way to the appointment with Mr Morgan. They didn't see her and she didn't bother to make her presence known. Time enough for that later, she thought.

Casualty was fairly slack that afternoon so Megan forced herself to take the opportunity to catch up with some paperwork. She had a lecture to give the following week to some pupil nurses and she needed to write up some transparencies to use for illustration on the overhead projector in the seminar room. It was a job she hated doing, but it had to be done and it needed all her concentration. So it was in a slightly irritated tone of voice that she answered the tentative knock on her door.

"Come in," she said without looking up.

"Hi," said a voice.

Megan looked up swiftly. It was Joanna, grinning like a Cheshire cat as she hobbled on her walking plaster towards Megan's desk.

Megan stood up and pushed her chair back. "Hello," she said, "you are looking very fit and well — obviously the leg isn't bothering you at all."

"No, it is absolutely fine," said Joanna, kissing Megan on both cheeks. "Mr Morgan says I can probably have the plaster off a week early." She sat down in the armchair. "Dad's just coming, he's still talking to Mr Morgan."

Megan perched herself on the edge of her desk. "I understand I am to convince your aunt that Earlsfield School is a good school for young ladies like you," she said.

Joanna grinned. "Don't worry, I think I've almost convinced her myself. She only needs a little push in the right direction."

"And I'm supposed to give that little

push?" queried Megan.

"That's the general idea," answered Joanna.

"Whose idea?" Megan couldn't resist asking. "Yours or your father's?"

"Both," came a deep voice from the doorway.

Megan stood up hastily and self-consciously smoothed her uniform, acutely aware of his steely blue gaze on her.

He smiled. "Why is it all nurses smooth their uniforms?" he said. "You look impeccable as usual." His blue eyes twinkled and Megan found herself smiling back against her will.

"It's a habit, I suppose," she said. "Something that lingers on from student days, when one was always being told off for some little thing."

"Joanna has told you that she is making excellent progress I suppose?" he said.

Megan laughed. "Yes, something about taking the plaster off a week early, I believe."

"That remains to be seen," said Giles. "I've been talking to Mr Morgan about that and we'll see after the next X-ray."

"Dad, honestly!" protested Joanna. "You treat me as if I'm a china doll. Are you like this with all your patients?"

"Yes," answered her father sternly. "I believe in erring on the side of caution." Joanna glowered at him but said nothing as Giles continued, "I've made a booking for a meal tonight for seven-thirty — will that suit you, Megan?"

"That will be fine," answered Megan, suddenly feeling self-conscious again. "What time will you pick me up?"

"At seven o'clock," said Giles matter-of-factly. "That will give us a short time for introductions and a drink before the meal." He looked at his watch. "Come along, you lady," he said to his daughter. "You and I are due back." He smiled briefly at Megan as they left the office. "See you at seven."

Megan nodded mutely. From seeming relaxed and friendly when he had first come in, he now seemed to have withdrawn again. I know this evening is going to be awful, thought Megan. I'm going to feel such an outsider. I wish I hadn't agreed to go. But she had, and she couldn't get out of it at that late stage, so that was that.

At seven promptly she was waiting outside the nurses' block. She had cursed herself for not asking Giles where they would be dining, but had guessed that it would be somewhere fairly expensive and had dressed accordingly. She had bought herself a new soft blue woollen dress before Christmas and had then forgotten to take it home with her and so had not worn it. Now seems a suitable opportunity she had thought as she got ready that evening. It was completely plain, a slim, knitted dress that clung to her shapely figure. With it she wore a simple gold locket as her only adornment. Her abundant brown hair she brushed back loosely and left it hanging in soft curls around her shoulders. She had been going to put it up, but remembering the last time she had dined with Giles she left it down. But why? a mocking little voice inside her taunted. It isn't going to be just the two of you alone this time, is it?

She had only waited a moment when Giles' car drew up silently alongside her. To her surprise it was empty save for Giles.

"But where are the others?" she asked.

"Waiting for us back at the hotel," answered Giles smoothly in a non-committal voice as he opened the car door for Megan. "As Fiona is staying at The Royal, and the food is good, I thought we might as well eat there. Fiona prefers hotel restaurants to other types of eating places anyway."

"Oh," said Megan, not knowing what else to say. The Royal was the most expensive hotel in town and she was glad she had worn her new dress, but

281

wished she'd had a smarter coat to put on. "I'm not looking terribly smart for The Royal," she said, indicating her old brown velvet coat. "I wore it for warmth."

"Very sensible," said Giles in the same non-committal tone of voice.

Oh hell, thought Megan despondently, this is going to be an awful evening, I just know it is.

She was sure the attendant at The Royal took her coat disdainfully as she handed it to him in the cloakroom, and it made her even more despondent. A fact not helped when she first set eyes on Fiona, Giles' sister-in-law. Megan had expected her to be attractive, but she had not expected her to be like something out of a fashion magazine. She was exquisitely groomed, from the pale golden hair on her head, down to the delicately painted toenails that peeped through the sheerest stockings out of impossibly high sandals. Suddenly the blue dress, which Megan had thought looked quite attractive, paled into insignificance. I might as well have got it from Oxfam thought Megan sourly, I can't compete with glamour like this.

"So nice to meet you, my dear, I've heard such a lot about you," Fiona drawled with a heavy American accent.

Megan smiled and extended her hand. "It's nice to meet you," she said briefly.

"Darling, do go and get us all a gin," Fiona said imperiously to Giles. Then turning back to Megan she asked, "Or would you prefer a Martini or something?"

Megan shook her head. "Gin and tonic will be fine." This was a Giles she hadn't seen before. Somehow she had never imagined him being ordered about by a woman, but he just nodded at Fiona and went across to the bar.

"I suppose you know why we've dragged you here," said Fiona, lighting a cigarette.

Megan nodded, watching with

fascination as her fingers with their incredibly long, red-painted nails cupped around the cigarette she was lighting. "Yes, you want to know about Earlsfield School," she said. "As I told Giles, it is some time since I left but I have kept in touch through various functions."

Fiona laughed and it was a low, sexy sound. "Some time since you left! My dear, you look as if you left yesterday. I find it incredible to think you are actually a Sister at the hospital."

"Well, she is, Aunt Fiona," interrupted Joanna, "and a very good one too."

"Yes, yes, I know, your father is always telling me," said her aunt. Then she patted Joanna on the hand. "Don't look so worried, I'm not going to upset your friend.

As the evening wore on Megan actually began to quite like Fiona. She was amusing, in a bitchy kind of way, and was quite obviously a woman of the world. Giles was strangely quiet though, and Megan wondered whether it was because she was there. He would probably prefer to be with Fiona on his own she thought, watching him as he was speaking to her. What was going on inside that handsome dark head of his? He seemed to be friendly and yet aloof, but Megan noticed that whatever Fiona wanted he ordered immediately.

By the end of the evening Fiona announced to the table at large that she was satisfied that Earlsfield School would be a suitable place for her niece to be educated. "Although I do make one stipulation," she said to Giles across the dinner table.

Megan glanced at Giles and saw his face harden. His mouth was tight as he answered, "Oh, and what is that?"

"That Joanna spends the long summer holidays with me. The Californian sunshine will do her good."

"Yes," Joanna answered, "I don't mind coming over for six weeks. That would be fun, as long as you promise we can go to the beach house."

"I promise," said Fiona, pulling a face, "as long as *you* promise you don't expect me to keep you company and lie out in the sun with you. The sun is so ageing to one's skin, don't you think?" she said turning to Megan.

"Why, I . . . er, I hadn't ever thought about it," said Megan truthfully. Now that she looked at Fiona closely she could see that she wasn't quite as flawless as she first appeared. Skilfully applied make-up hid her faults.

"No," said Fiona with a little laugh, "I don't suppose you have. When you are as young as you are, you don't have to worry about lines and wrinkles."

"Oh, I never will," answered Megan emphatically. "If the wrinkles come, let them. Laughter lines, that's what my mother always call them."

"Character lines," said Giles.

Fiona glanced at him, annoyance written all over her face. "If Giles had his way, women would go without make-up altogether," she said.

In that brief moment Megan caught a glimpse of the relationship between Giles and Fiona. They were obviously both strong characters and she knew instinctively that they must have clashed head-on over something. Still, that doesn't always stop you loving someone she thought, remembering what Giles had said about not being able to switch off love. They were closely tied, she could see it, and the thought rankled. It's no good, she thought bitterly. Much as I love him, I could never play second fiddle to that fascinating creature. That is, even if he asked me! He'll never find another woman like her, and certainly an uninteresting little hospital sister, who has done nothing special and been nowhere in particular, can ever hope to take her place.

As soon as they had finished their coffee Megan made her excuses. "Thank you for a lovely dinner," she said politely to Giles. "It was nice meeting you, Fiona, and I'm glad if I've been able to help."

"You have, my dear," drawled Fiona, extending her long white hand tipped with the blood-red nails. "I feel satisfied in my own mind now." She smiled at Megan. "Perhaps I'll see you again some time."

"Perhaps," said Megan, resisting the temptation to add, *but it's highly unlikely*!

Giles rose with Megan. "I'll get your coat," he said, "and then I'll drive you back to the hospital."

Megan protested. "That isn't necessary, I can take a taxi, it's no problem."

"It's no problem for me to drive you either," he said brusquely. "I'll get your coat." Without waiting for her reply he strode across to the cloakroom.

On the drive back they engaged in a stilted form of conversation. Megan felt miserable; he was so near and yet so far away . . . His thoughts were still with Fiona, she supposed sadly. She longed to reach out and touch his stern profile, but knew she daren't however much she wanted to.

"I'll be glad when Richard starts his term again," she said for want of something better to say. "At least then I'll have my car back again."

"Yes," said Giles, "you'll be able to get out and about with your friends."

"Oh, I do that anyway," replied Megan without thinking and then stopped, remembering when he had telephoned and Johnny had answered.

"I'm aware of that," said Giles smoothly, his voice sounding cold and hard.

Megan felt even more miserable. It was bad enough her loving him and him not being particularly interested, but somehow the fact that he thought she was having an affair with Johnny Cox made it even more unbearable. Yet what could she do? It would be quite ridiculous for her to tell him that Johnny and Susan were the ones who had fallen in love — he wouldn't be interested. Even worse, he might guess the reason she wanted him to know. But in spite of logic telling her otherwise, Megan rashly decided to take the plunge.

"Johnny Cox isn't my boyfriend, you know," she remarked as casually as her voice would allow. "He's very smitten with Susan North and I wouldn't be surprised if they got engaged soon."

Giles turned and looked at her with a strange expression in his blue eyes. "Oh, I'm sorry Megan," he said.

"Why?" asked Megan, not expecting this reaction from him.

"I don't like to think of you being hurt," he said quietly.

"Johnny hasn't hurt me," said Megan emphatically. "He has only ever been a plain, ordinary friend to me, nothing more, and I'm glad for him and Susan."

"I see," said Giles. "I must have been mistaken then, but from what Richard said, or rather, perhaps *didn't* say, I gathered that he thought there was someone rather special in your life."

There is, there is, it's you, Megan wanted to cry out, but all she said, in an almost inaudible whisper, was,

"There is, but nothing will ever come of it."

"Why not?" demanded Giles.

"Because . . . " Megan hesitated. How could she get out of this hole without letting him guess the true identity of the man she loved. "It's too complicated and anyway it wouldn't interest you," she said at last rather lamely.

"Oh," said Giles. Then he said, "The course of true love never does run smoothly, so they tell me."

How well I know it thought Megan, but said nothing as Giles brought the big car to a halt outside the nurses' home.

"Thank you once again for a pleasant evening," she said, her voice sounding small and tight in her ears. She felt like an awkward schoolgirl, groping for the right words.

"Thank you for convincing Fiona," he said. "The evening went very smoothly I thought."

"Oh yes," said Megan quickly, "I

liked Fiona and she's very glamorous, isn't she?"

"Yes," said Giles abruptly and in a tone of voice that precluded any further conversation. "Goodnight, Megan." He leaned across and opened the car door for her. As he moved, the weight of his body brushed against her. Megan felt her senses drowning as she smelled the heady odour of his aftershave, the tangy masculine fragrance of his skin. She longed to brush her lips against his dark head and put her arms around him.

He turned to her as he drew back from opening the door and for a moment Megan thought her dreams were to be answered and that he would kiss her, for his face came nearer to hers. She could just see the rugged outline of his features in the semi-darkness and she felt herself being drawn towards him as if he was a powerful magnet. It seemed to Megan that they lingered like that for a lifetime, quivering on the brink of a kiss. Then swiftly he drew back.

"I must get back to Joanna and Fiona," he said.

"Yes," said Megan dully, "you must." She climbed out of the car, her heart a leaden weight of pain. She could have cried out loud in her anguish, but instead she managed a bright smile and a wave as she closed the door.

"Thank you again for a lovely dinner," she said, slamming the door shut.

Giles just nodded briefly in acknowledgement and then, putting the car in gear, roared off into the darkness without a backward glance.

10

AFTER that evening with Giles, Fiona and Joanna, it seemed to Megan that he was avoiding her. Rubbish, it's your imagination she told herself — he has no reason to avoid you. Whatever the reason, however, their paths hardly crossed at all in the following week. He only came into the casualty area when a senior opinion was needed, and even Casualty itself was strangely quiet.

"Boring, isn't it?" said Thelma to Megan one day. "Usually I'm rushed off my feet and curse people who come in here with trivial complaints, but at the moment I'd welcome a case of sunburn!"

Megan laughed. "Welcome it? I should think we'd all be amazed by it! Particularly as it's the end of January and we haven't seen the sun for at least eight days!" She sighed. "Everything has been hidden by this depressing grey cloud and it just suits my mood."

"Mine too," said Thelma gloomily.

"What about your philosophy of always looking on the bright side?" asked Megan. "What has happened to that?"

"Gone down the plughole," said Thelma, "along with the washing-up water."

"You must get yourself a dishwasher then," said Jamie Green as he breezed in, white coat flying behind him.

"Where have you been?" asked Megan. "I haven't seen you since the Christmas show. I kept meaning to ask where you were but I forgot."

"Just shows how unimportant I am," said Jamie. "And there was I, thinking that Casualty couldn't manage without me."

"It was very difficult, dear," said Thelma brightening. Jamie had always been one of her favourites. "How did the study leave go?" she asked. "And more importantly, how did the exam go?"

"Well, the written wasn't too bad, but I've still got the horror of the vivas to survive. Still," he added, "if all else fails I can always be an ambulance driver, or better still a train driver. That always was my original ambition!"

Megan laughed. "You won't fail, I'm sure," she said. For all his joking and seemingly flippant attitude, Jamie Green was an extremely serious and dedicated young doctor, and she was sure he would make it to the top.

"Better go and see the big white boss I suppose," said Jamie. "He gave me strict instructions to report back to him after the exam, and he wants a copy of the paper." He fished a crumpled piece of paper with printed questions on it out of his pocket.

"That's a bit mucky," said Megan. "If you photocopy it, at least you can give Mr Elliott a flat copy and not one that looks as if it has been used to wrap fish and chips."

"Probably was," said Jamie. "I don't remember much of last night. After the exam I went out on the town with some old mates of mine from medical school." He laughed. "Do you know, one of them is still up in London — he can't remember where he left his car!"

"I don't believe you," cried Megan and Thelma simultaneously.

"It's true," insisted Jamie. "He had to ring his department at Northampton and tell them he was sick. He daren't say he was too drunk to remember where he had put the car."

"I should think not," said Megan severely. "That wouldn't go down at all well with his superiors. Here, give me that," she took the scruffy exam paper from Jamie. "I'll pop along to the photocopier and copy it for you before you go in to see Mr Elliott." With the exam paper in her hand she hurried off down the corridor towards the admin block where the photocopier was located. As she passed

Giles Elliott's office the door opened and he strode out. A collision was inevitable for Megan was going down the corridor fast and Giles had his head down reading some notes. As she cannoned into him Megan knocked the file from his hand, the folder split open and the patient's notes, records and letters spilled out everywhere on to the corridor floor.

Giles swore softly under his breath.

"Oh, I'm sorry," muttered Megan in confusion, bending down to pick up the papers at the very moment Giles also bent down for the same reason. Their faces came to within an inch of each other and Megan could feel the warmth of his breath on her cheek and dared not look up. If she looked into those blue eyes of his she would be lost, she knew it.

"Let's toss for it." His deep voice sounded amused. "If we both try and pick them up we shall bang heads and end up being treated for concussion."

Megan stood up, still not looking at

him. "I'd better pick them up as it was really my fault," she said, looking down at the floor.

"Nonsense, it was just as much my fault," he answered. "I wasn't looking where I was going," he laughed gently.

A secretary came out of the typists' office further down the corridor. "Oh, Mr Elliott," she said, "what a mess you've got those notes in!" She bent down and proceeded to pick up the papers and put them in order.

There was no reason to stay chatting any longer and Megan felt suddenly shy. It was his eyes; she felt sure he could read every chaotic thought that was tumbling through her head.

"I'd better be about my business," she muttered and started to walk down the corridor, acutely aware that he was standing watching her. She could feel his gaze on her back almost like a physical pressure. Thank goodness I wear tights and not seamed stockings like Thelma, she thought feverishly.

At least I know I haven't got crooked seams!

As she turned the corner into the admin block she breathed a huge sigh of relief. She hadn't seen him for days, then all it had needed was a brief encounter for her to feel like a lovesick sixteen-year-old again. She slapped the exam paper angrily against her side. You are stupid, Megan Jones, she told herself. It's just no good, you have got to stop caring about him. Although even as she was giving herself such good sensible advice she knew it was futile. She might just as well have been King Canute trying to hold back the waves.

She didn't see Giles again that day. Although she knew he was in his office because she could hear his voice every time she walked past, he didn't emerge again. As she went off duty that night Megan thought of the next two days ahead. Two whole days off, plus the weekend. Normally she looked forward to the times when she had a nice long stretch of off-duty. It didn't happen too often as she usually worked a normal week, Monday to Friday, but every now and then, because time off had accrued, she was able to have extra leave.

This particular time, however, she viewed the forthcoming four days with anything but enthusiasm. She knew she had to fill in the hours with activity, otherwise her mind would be filled with thoughts of Giles Elliott. That wretched man, she thought angrily, but she was angry with herself, not him.

After she had changed out of her uniform and had a coffee, she suddenly made up her mind on the spur of the moment to drive back down to Devon to see her mother. Better ring her, I suppose, she thought as she flung a few things into a suitcase, knowing Mrs Jones would appreciate some advance notice.

Her mother was delighted, if a little surprised, at the unexpected prospect of having her daughter home for four days. "It will be lovely to have you to myself, dear," she said. "We can have a good long chat, like we used to in the old days." She paused a moment. "There's nothing wrong, is there, dear?"

"No, of course not," answered Megan brightly. "I don't come often enough. I'm just making the most of an unexpected opportunity. Is it all right if I drive down tonight?" she added.

"Tonight!" Her mother was surprised. "Well, all right, dear, if that's what you want to do. I'll have supper waiting for you and we'll have it in the kitchen together in front of the old wood stove. I lit it today for a change; I must have had a premonition that you were coming!"

Megan's face brightened at the thought of sitting in the big old kitchen in front of the stove. She had always done that as a child, only then everything had seemed so cosy and secure. No disturbing thoughts of a tall dark man to trouble her serenity in those far-off days.

The journey down was quicker than Megan had expected. The roads were almost completely traffic free and it seemed no time at all before she was sitting with her mother and sipping home-made broth in front of the warm stove.

Megan wriggled her toes comfortably towards the heat. "This is lovely," she said. "Sitting here like this makes me think I must be mad existing in that wretched little room at the hospital. I must do something about moving out."

"Where will you move to?" asked her mother practically.

"Oh, I don't know. Perhaps I'll try to get a small mortgage on something when this house is paid for — that's not long now."

Her mother snorted. "The prices they ask these days for houses is ridiculous. All you would be able to afford would be a little tiny box on an estate, and somehow I don't think you'd like that."

"At least I'd have a little more room," protested Megan.

"A little, but not much," said her mother decisively, and Megan knew she was right. She would never be able to afford anything spacious. "Anyway," Mrs Jones continued, "Why buy something yourself? You will probably get married one day and you can pool some of your money with your husband and buy a better house.

Megan sighed and pushed her empty plate away on the scrubbed wood of the kitchen table. Then she stretched slowly and luxuriously in the warmth from the stove. "Mum," she said sleepily, "if I wait until I get married, I'll still be living in that hospital room when I'm ninety."

"No you won't," said her mother, ever practical. "You'll have to retire at sixty!"

Megan laughed and reached over and patted her affectionately on the knee. "I'll be living in some retired nurses' home then," she said, "in an equally depressing little room."

"Oh, Megan," said her mother crossly, "you *are* silly! Of *course* you'll get married."

"Nobody has asked me yet," pointed out Megan, "and you do need a man in the picture somewhere; it's essential, you know."

"There is one in the picture already," said her mother. "Only you don't seem to be doing much to encourage him."

"What do you mean?" asked Megan, looking at her, her large, expressive brown eyes startled.

"I mean Giles Elliott of course," said Mrs Jones. "It's quite obvious he is more than a little interested in you, but you don't seem to help — you blow hot and cold where he is concerned."

"I certainly don't blow hot and cold," said Megan quickly, "*he* . . . " She stopped. She had been about to blurt out the fact that he was the one who seemed to blow hot and cold, but then that would be admitting that she was still in love with him. "His sister-in-law, Fiona, seems to be very much in the picture," she said calmly. "I'm afraid you have got the wrong idea where he is concerned."

"I don't think so," said her mother stubbornly. "I always go by my intuition."

"Mum," said Megan wearily, "we have discussed him before, remember? And we ended up arguing, so don't let's do it again."

Her mother looked obstinate and for a moment Megan thought she was going to pursue the subject, but then she smiled and squeezed Megan's hand. "You're right," she said. "Come on, it's late, time for bed for both of us. Of course," she added casually, "there is one lesson to be learned from Giles Elliott."

Megan frowned; what was she getting at? "What?" she asked.

"It's a great mistake to marry young. I hope Richard thinks of that and gets over his crush on Joanna."

Megan laughed. "I shouldn't worry about Richard, he's got his head screwed on the right way — and anyway, how do you know Giles married young?"

"He told me," said her mother airily. "Of course, they were both students at the time and I gather she was pregnant."

Megan stared at her. "You mean his wife?" she said.

"Of course I mean his wife," said her mother. "Who else is Joanna's mother?"

"Oh!" Megan choked back the feeling of resentment that rose within her. Why should she resent the fact that they had found pleasure in each other before marriage? It was none of her business, but somehow it hurt her more than she dare admit to herself. "I'm off to bed then," she said, forcing a bright smile to her lips. "Goodnight, Mum." She made her way up the polished oak stairs to her room before her mother could shatter her with any more revelations.

She lay in bed, miserable tears trickling down her cheeks and soaking the fine linen of the pillowcase. Stop it, you fool, she whispered to herself. You are behaving totally irrationally. It doesn't matter what happened in his life before, it's now that matters. That was the trouble though. Fiona was there to remind him, and she was so attractive. Surely, *surely* Giles must be drawn to her, and not only because they had a common bond in the care of Joanna. Even though they obviously did argue, Megan felt that Fiona had a hold over Giles, a power, something she couldn't quite understand, and certainly something she would never have.

She fished out a clean handkerchief from underneath her pillow. Rather the opposite, she thought ruefully, blowing her nose vigorously. He is the one who has the hold; he holds you in the palm of his hand like a malleable piece of clay. Oh Giles, I do love you and I wish I didn't, she murmured as at last she fell into a troubled and disturbed sleep.

Next day Megan and her mother decided to drive into Exeter and do some shopping, although Mrs Jones did ask her daughter if she wanted to go. "You look quite peaky, dear," she said, looking at her with concern. "Are you all right?"

"Perhaps I've got a cold coming," said Megan. Her eyes did look a bit pink she knew, and a cold was a good excuse. "The fresh air will do me good."

They had a lovely morning and ended up staying for lunch at a little restaurant in an ancient building alongside the cathedral. Megan was thankful that her mother didn't mention Giles Elliott again, and she was careful to keep the conversation well away from anything to do with the hospital. Mrs Jones, for her part, seemed more than content to chatter on, making sure that Megan caught up with all the local gossip.

As they were leaving they bumped

into an old school-friend of Megan's. Her name was Jean and she had two small blonde children in tow, a small boy of about four and a toddler, obviously a girl as she was dressed from head to toe in pink.

"Gracious, what a long time it is since I saw you!" Jean exclaimed. "Megan, you don't look a day older, just as glamorous." She glanced down at her shabby clothes. "You make me feel very scruffy, but I'm afraid all our money goes on these two." She gazed down proudly at her children.

Megan smiled. "I can see they are both the apple of your eye," she said. "You're very lucky, Jean, to have two such beautiful children."

Jean beamed at the compliment. "Yes, although I admit I am rather biased — they are lovely, aren't they?" She laughed happily.

On the way home Megan couldn't get Jean and her two lovely children out of her thoughts. Here she was, the same age as Jean, but a childless spinster.

Yes, that's what I am she thought vehemently, a childless spinster, and that's how I am going to end up!

"A penny for them," said her mother, who was driving.

"What?" asked Megan, startled out of her black mood.

"Penny for your thoughts," said her mother. "You've been completely silent ever since we left Exeter."

"Have I?" said Megan. "Sorry, I wasn't thinking about anything in particular." She was lying of course, but she couldn't possibly confess what her thoughts had really been.

Although she tried hard to shake it off, Megan found the pervading sense of gloom enveloping her. The more and more she thought about it, suddenly the more she felt that she had wasted her life, that she had missed something. It was strange; she had never given such things a thought before. Nursing had been her life — it had been filled with everything she had thought necessary. She had never felt the slightest desire to be married and have a family. In fact she had always secretly felt sorry for her friends who had got married. She'd always thought of them as being tied and of herself as being free but now suddenly she wondered if perhaps it was the reverse. They were tied, it was true, but they were tied to people, to a family, to something that was a lasting entity, an on-going thing. Whereas she was tied to nothing more than a job.

Oh true, she tried to convince herself, it was a worth-while job, but patients came and went and although she knew she helped them and that they were grateful, she very rarely ever saw them again, and it was not possible to form lasting relationships with them or even really with one's colleagues. The hospital staff was composed of a shifting population; junior doctors had limited contracts and had to move away for their training, and nurses! She sighed; well, they either moved on, got married, or a few stayed and stayed until they retired — and if I'm not careful that will be me, thought Megan.

That night when she was sitting with her mother after dinner watching television, Megan said casually, "You know, I've been thinking."

"Really dear!" said her mother, the irony in her tone passing unnoticed by Megan.

"Yes," said Megan, sitting on the settee with her knees hunched up under her chin. "I've got into a rut. I think it's about time I did something about it."

Her mother raised her eyebrows. "Well, dear, at your tender age I would hardly say you were in a rut," she murmured. "But never mind, tell me what you are planning."

"I think I must move," said Megan positively. "I must either apply for a nursing officer's post or I must take a nursing job abroad."

"I see," said Mrs Jones slowly, looking at Megan carefully. "What has made you suddenly decide this?"

"Oh, it isn't really sudden," answered Megan, getting up restlessly and going over to the window. Looking out into the dense blackness of the night it seemed to her for a fanciful moment that she was looking into her own soul, dense and black, completely unknown to her. "I've been thinking about it for some time," she continued casually. "I can't stay a Sister in Casualty for ever, you know."

"Yes, but you'll . . . "

Megan swung round and interrupted her mother fiercely. "Don't say I'll get married," she said quickly. "That does *not* feature in my plans! When it does I'll be the first to tell you." She drew the curtains together in an irritable movement, which did not go unnoticed by her mother. "No, I've got to do something more positive with my life. I'm going to start job hunting."

Mrs Jones patted the settee beside her. "Come and sit down and relax at least for now," she said. "You know I'll support you in whatever you want to do." She smiled at Megan. "If you do get a job on the other side of the world, I'll be able to come and visit you."

Megan looked at her. Although her mother hadn't said so, she knew she would miss her terribly if she went to some far-off place; and what was more, in spite of all her brave words Megan knew she would miss England terribly. Perhaps I should try for a nursing officer's post, she thought, but she knew whatever she did it would have to be somewhere other than the County General. She just couldn't go on working in a place where she was likely to run into Giles Elliott any moment of the day.

"Don't worry, Mum," she said hugging her, "I don't think I could bear to move too far away from Devon. I'm a country girl at heart."

"You must do what you think is right for you," said her mother, knitting vigorously. "Just as long as you are happy."

"Oh Mum," Megan flung her arms around her, "I wish I could be calm like you."

"Megan," grumbled Mrs Jones, "you've made me drop a stitch." Then she added slowly as she carefully retrieved the dropped stitch, "My calmness hasn't come easily to me you know; it comes from years of practice."

Megan laughed. "Yes, I can believe that," she said. "I think I'd better start practising now. In the meantime," she got up and went across to the sideboard, "how about us both having a nice glass of sherry?"

"Good idea," said her mother, "there's plenty left over from Christmas. Giles was so generous I've got enough drink left to last me the rest of the year."

At the mention of Giles' name, Megan paused momentarily, sherry bottle in her hand. The image of his darkly handsome face flashed up in front of her. Why is it there is always something to remind me of him? she thought as she poured the clear golden liquid into the cut-glass sherry glasses.

"I'll go and buy the *Nursing Mirror* tomorrow," she said, handing her mother the glass of sherry. "It's the beginning of a new year, a good time to make a new start."

"Yes, dear," said her mother, quietly sipping the sherry. From the tone of her voice Megan knew she was not convinced that it was a good idea!

The days passed quickly. Megan went for long walks along the beach she loved and knew so well. The biting fresh air did her good and she felt strengthened in her resolve to make a move from the County General. It seemed that she had only just arrived when Sunday morning came, and after lunch she would have to pack up and drive back to the hospital.

"Are you going for your morning constitutional?" asked her mother.

Megan laughed. "You make me sound as if I'm about ninety! That's what old people do, take their morning constitutional!"

"I didn't mean it like that," smiled Mrs Jones. "You know what I mean. I'll cook lunch and you go for a walk along the beach, I know you love it there."

So Megan did; she strode along the beach, the keen sea air bringing a delicate colour to her cheeks, her long dark hair streaming out in the wind behind her. Once again, as she had done so many times before, she thought how beautiful was the scene before her. The wide stretch of the waters of the estuary, today whipped up by the wind, foaming white horses tipping the tops of the waves. The patchwork of the countryside across the water appearing mistily through the fine haze thrown up by the foam, like a delicate water-colour.

The gulls swooped and dived, their plaintive screams torn to shreds by the wind and tossed to the elements. Megan felt exhilarated and she began to run, flinging her arms up to the sky. There was no one there to see her, the beach was deserted. At least she thought so, until she suddenly saw the tall figure of a man making his way down the sand dunes that sloped steeply at the back of the beach. He was some distance away, but near enough for Megan to know that he must have seen her running like a child, her arms thrown wide to the winds. She stopped dead in her tracks, embarrassed, hoping it wasn't someone she knew.

Then her heart stopped and she felt a sinking feeling in the pit of her stomach. The distinctive long stride, the height, the dark hair . . . It couldn't be, it wasn't possible, but she knew it was. It was Giles Elliott making his way along the beach towards her.

If this was a film, thought Megan almost hysterically, we would be running towards each other gracefully with our arms outstretched, and it would all be in slow motion. We'd have ecstatic expressions on our faces as we were running, and when we met we would wrap our arms around each other and kiss passionately! However, as it was, she stood uncertainly not knowing what to do, drawing a pattern in the firm sand with the toe of her shoe. She could hear his voice now, calling, "Megan!" It sounded plaintive as it mingled with the calls of the gulls. Slowly she began to walk towards him. Why ever was he here? Was something wrong?

The concern must have shown on her face because he said with a laugh, as soon as he reached her, "Don't look so perturbed, there's nothing sinister in my being here."

"But why are you here?" demanded Megan. "You're the very last person I expected to run into here."

"Run into being the operative word," he smiled. "I saw you running as if you hadn't a care in the world."

"Perhaps I was running away from my cares," said Megan soberly. "But that doesn't answer my question — why are you here?"

"I had a free day and I thought about this lovely part of the country, and on impulse I decided to come down and take your mother out to lunch." He grinned ruefully. "Of course, acting in a typically masculine fashion, I didn't think to ring and ask first whether or not it would be convenient." He took Megan's arm. "However, your mother being the splendid woman she is, has taken it all in her stride and invited me to lunch."

Megan wanted to take her arm away from his. The simple intimate gesture of drawing her arm to link with his hurt so much, for it meant nothing to him she knew; being so close to him was a physical pain for her.

"Where are Fiona and Joanna?" she asked as calmly as her turbulent emotions would allow.

"Spending the weekend together. Fiona returns to the States tomorrow and on Wednesday Joanna starts at her new school." He smiled at her, a smile that made her feel as if suddenly it was summer. "Thanks to you, I can start to settle down at last," he said. "As soon as Joanna starts school I shall begin house-hunting. I was going to ask you to help me, but your mother tells me you are thinking of moving on."

Megan wondered what else her mother had said. She hoped she hadn't tried her hand at matchmaking. But no, whatever she might think, Megan knew she could rely on her to be tactful.

"Is it true?" asked Giles. "Are you really going to leave the County General?"

"I've got to find another job first," answered Megan, avoiding his searching blue eyes. "I shall be around for a little while yet, unless of course I'm very lucky and the right job turns up suddenly."

"This is all a bit sudden, isn't it?" asked Giles. "You seemed content before with the work at the County General. What has changed to make you alter your mind?"

"Nothing," lied Megan miserably. How could she say, *You've changed everything for me*? "Of course," she made her voice sound as matter of fact as possible, "I shall be looking for a job with a higher salary."

Giles stopped suddenly and, pulling on her arm, turned her round to face him. "You're not short of money, are you?" he asked. "For your brother and mother I mean, because if you are you know I would be only too willing to help."

Megan flushed brick red with embarrassment. "No, it's not that," she mumbled uncomfortably. "I just think it's about time I moved on, that's all." His generous gesture touched and embarrassed her. "It's kind of you to offer to help though," she said softly. "I appreciate your thoughtfulness to my family."

"I . . . " he hesitated, then said, "Well, that's all right then, but just remember, if you ever do need help, don't hesitate to come to me."

"I'll remember," said Megan, still not daring to look at him.

"You wouldn't come to me though, would you?" he said. Although he said it almost as a statement rather than a question.

Megan hung her head. "I'd find it difficult," she admitted. Then almost defiantly she faced him squarely. "But then I'd find it difficult to ask favours from anyone."

"You shouldn't find it difficult to ask friends favours," he said. "I asked you a favour, and you've done me a tremendous service where Joanna is concerned. You've no idea of the burden you've lifted from my shoulders now that I know she can stay here and everything is amicably settled. You helped to make things easier for me with Fiona."

Hot prickles of resentment crept along Megan's spine at his mention of Fiona. It seemed she would always come between them.

"I know Fiona may seem a bit hard on the surface," continued Giles, "but for all her faults she does love Joanna, and I know she is happy to leave Joanna here knowing that someone like you is in the background. Someone a young girl can turn to if she needs anyone. So you see," he drew Megan close, "I want you to stay at the County General for Joanna's sake."

"Even if I move from the County General," stammered Megan, her lips trembling at his closeness, "I won't be at the other end of the earth. I could never go very far away from Devon so Joanna would always be able to find me."

"And would I be able to find you too?" asked Giles softly, bending slowly towards her. Megan inclined her face to meet his mouth as his lips came down on hers with a lingering passion. Her hands instinctively flew up to his shoulders, clasping them, drawing him closer to her. The drumming of her own pulses in her ears deafened her,

her mouth trembled beneath his as she felt her whole body go limp with desire.

Giles drew back from the kiss slowly, his strong mouth curved in a gentle smile. "I want you so much, Megan," he whispered, "and it's not only for Joanna's sake."

As if in a dream Megan locked her hands behind his head, tangling her fingers in his thick dark hair. "Giles, I want you too," she whispered, "but I thought you weren't interested."

"How could you think that?" He smiled as his lips traced a blazing trail along the outline of her jaw. "You're skin is as soft as silk," he murmured when he reached the pulsating hollow of her throat.

Megan trembled and tears of exquisite joy wet her long silky lashes; this was everything she had dreamed of and more. One moment she had been alone on the beach, the next moment she was in Giles' arms and he was saying everything she had ever longed to hear.

"Megan, don't leave the County General," he said, his warm lips nibbling her ear lobe. "Stay there, so that I can see you as often as I like."

A painful doubt began to flood Megan's heart. She had been on the point of revealing that she loved him, but something had held it back. Now she was glad. He had only said he wanted her, nothing about loving her, and now he implied that all he wanted was for her to be available, to stay at the County General so that he could see her whenever he liked. Whenever *he* liked; to make use of her, in other words. Not the kind of relationship Megan had in mind with Giles Elliott or any other man.

She drew back, pushing him away with hands that only a few moments before had been pulling him closer so eagerly. "I can't let sentiment for any man get in the way of my career," she said sharply. She knew she was over-reacting, but she couldn't help it, her emotions were a raw mixture of love, hate and jealousy.

Love, because try as she might she had to acknowledge that she loved him, but hate and jealousy too, even though she despised herself for letting such stupid irrational emotions overwhelm her. She put up a barrier between herself and her seething emotions, between herself and Giles Elliott.

Giles looked at her when she spoke with something akin to astonishment on his face. "I thought you said just now that you wanted me?" he said, a note of incredulous anger creeping into his voice.

"I did," said Megan, disengaging herself completely from his embrace, "but as I said before, I'm not going to let emotion get in the way of my career."

"But the way you kissed me!" said Giles.

"A momentary lapse," insisted Megan airily, her voice sounding surprisingly firm in her ears. "Suddenly you were there, you kissed me and I responded. A perfectly natural reaction, I'm sure you would agree!" She started to walk briskly back along the sand towards the house. "Come on, unless you want to get cut off by the tide."

"I think I already have been," muttered Giles. "I don't understand you, Megan, I thought you liked me."

"I do like you," said Megan, "but that doesn't stop me from wanting to change my job."

Angrily Giles pulled her back, preventing her from walking on. "Why doesn't it?" he demanded. "Why can't you stay where you can be near me?"

"I was not put on this earth for your convenience," snapped Megan, beginning to get angry at his persistence. "If our paths cross that will be nice, but as I said before I can't let sentiment stand in my way."

"I've made a mistake about you," muttered Giles under his breath. "I didn't realise you were so hard."

"Just as well you found out in time

then," said Megan curtly and began walking again. This time Giles didn't try to stop her but just strode along in silence beside her. Megan had difficulty in keeping back the stinging tears that threatened to come. Pretending to be a hard woman was difficult, but she was determined not to let him see how much he had hurt her by just asking her to be around.

No, damn it, she thought defiantly, every female instinct to the fore as she strode ahead, her dark hair blowing behind her like a defiant banner in the wind — I shall keep my pride intact, if nothing else!

11

LUNCH was a difficult affair to say the least, and as far as Megan was concerned it couldn't go by fast enough. She did her best to be bright and cheerful and she noticed Giles was making a determined effort too. We should have both been actors she thought sourly; we'd be nominated for Oscars for our performances todays! The one thing she was thankful for was that at least they appeared to have fooled her mother.

She was in her element with two extra people to Sunday lunch, and as usual she had turned an ordinary lunch into a gourmet feast of roast beef, fluffy Yorkshire pudding, crunchy roast potatoes and parsnips, sprouts and thick, tasty gravy.

"It's just as well I don't see you too often, Mrs Jones," remarked Giles, pushing his plate away. "I should very soon put on weight and have to go on a diet."

"Nonsense," said Mrs Jones briskly. "You are one of the lean kind, you'll stay just the way you are all your life. Have a little more." But try as she might she couldn't persuade him.

"I only intended this to be a brief visit," he said, "and of course I didn't know Megan was here, otherwise I wouldn't have inflicted myself upon you. I'd better be getting back now and leave you two together for an hour. I take it you have got your car here, Megan?" He looked directly at her for the first time since their quarrel on the beach.

Megan returned his blue-eyed scrutiny calmly. "Yes, thanks, I have," she said and smiled. It was an empty smile she knew, and Giles knew too. A smile that only played about her lips but which had no warmth and never reached her large brown eyes. If he was looking for some sign that she had changed her mind he would be disappointed — and he always would be, she thought bitterly. I shall never be there waiting for you, at your beck and call, standing in the shadow of your glamorous sister-in-law, she resolved. What really was their relationship? The nasty little voice at the back of her mind would not be stilled, even though it was something Megan tried not to think about. However, the disturbing image of Giles and Fiona together, looking such an elegant pair, was never very far away.

After Giles had left Megan chattered on brightly, perhaps a little too brightly, telling her mother about Susan North and Johnny Cox, about Thelma and her rotten husband. In fact, about anything she could think of. She hardly let her mother get a word in edgeways, which was really the object of the exercise. The very last thing she wanted was for Mrs Jones to question her about Giles Elliott. If her mother was surprised at Megan's sudden loquaciousness, she didn't remark on it, just nodded and smiled and appeared to enjoy all the gossip which was kept up non-stop until the time came for Megan to leave.

As she drove back through the darkened countryside, Megan put her radio on full blast and drove at a furious pace. After a while, common sense took over and she slowed down. You're not driving away from him, she reflected ruefully, you're driving towards him — so why be in such a hurry! She would see him soon enough in the casualty department the next day, although she vowed she would try to keep out of his way as much as possible.

Monday morning in Casualty was busy and Megan was almost literally run off her feet. By skipping lunch altogether herself, she managed to see that all the junior nurses had a lunch-break. Hers consisted of a snatched cup of coffee in her office before she was back in the casualty receiving area. Monday was usually reasonably busy anyway, because Giles Elliott held a review clinic and all the patients who had presented with minor injuries over the weekend were reviewed by him on Monday morning, so that usually accounted for a fair number of people. But on this particular morning the casualty waiting area was bursting at the seams.

Megan had separated the patients into those for the review clinic and those waiting for treatment, which helped to simplify matters a little. She needn't have worried about embarrassing encounters with Giles because he was as busy as she was, closeted in his clinic, his secretary by his side taking the notes he dictated to the patients' GPs after he had seen each case.

It was only at the end of a long and arduous day that Megan remembered with an impending sense of panic that tomorrow she had to lecture to the pupil nurses and she still hadn't had time to rehearse her lecture with the transparencies. The temptation was to leave it, she felt so tired, but when she got to her office there were the transparencies lying on her desk and she knew she just had to put them on the overhead projector and run through her lecture.

Sighing, she collected her notes and the transparencies together. Might as well do it now, she thought resignedly, otherwise there'll be no sleep for you tonight, my girl.

Making her way down the corridor, she unlocked the seminar room attached to the accident and emergency department where all the lectures were given. At least she would be left in peace now. Juliet Moore had come on duty so no one would interrupt her.

Megan carefully lined up her transparencies and, putting one on the projector, switched it on. Adjusting the little magnifying glass that reflected the writing on to the large wall screen proved to be difficult. Megan struggled with it for half an hour, becoming more and more frustrated. The wretched

336

thing would not stay in the right place. She either had an enormous picture that would not fit the screen, or a tiny one which could only be reflected on the ceiling!

"I can see the whole damned thing is going to be a disaster," she muttered, speaking her vexed thoughts out loud.

"Is it?" asked a deep voice from the doorway.

Startled, Megan turned, the light from the overhead projector illuminating her slender body, but blinding her to the tall masculine figure standing in the doorway. Not that she needed any light to know it was Giles Elliott — the sound of his voice was enough.

Ignoring the thudding of her heart and steeling herself against any kind of emotion as best she could, Megan turned back to the projector.

"This wretched thing will not behave itself, and I've got to use it tomorrow."

"Here, let me see." Switching on the main light he came across to where she was standing. "What seems to be the trouble?" he asked.

Megan explained the problem. "I think the screws must be worn out," she said. "The ones that hold the magnifying glass in position."

"Hmmm," muttered Giles, looking at it intensely, "you are probably right, and it's too late now to get it mended today."

"I'll never get the maintenance department to do it in time for the lecture tomorrow," said Megan, a note of panic creeping into her voice. "They need a requisition about a fortnight in advance for any work they do."

Giles smiled, a wry twist to his lips. "Don't tell me our cool, calm, unemotional Sister Jones is panicking!" he said.

Megan ignored the jibe. "It doesn't matter," she said as calmly as possible, gathering her notes together. "I'll just have to borrow a projector from the school of nursing tomorrow morning early. I'll arrange it before the lecture."

"Hold your horses," said Giles,

fiddling with the screw. "I think we can make do and mend with this one, at least for tomorrow." He tore a piece of paper from a notepad which he took from his pocket, then he folded it into a very small square. "Now, if I wedge this in here I think that should do the trick," he said confidently, pushing the paper between the screw and the side of the glass. "Now let's see." He adjusted the magnifying glass so that the notes on the transparency were in perfect focus on the screen, then let go and the magnifying glass promptly fell down with a plop so that the transparency was reflected in miniature on the ceiling once more!

Megan restrained a wild impulse to giggle hysterically, for Giles looked annoyed at the fact that his brilliant strategy hadn't worked. "I think perhaps I'd better borrow a projector," she said.

He frowned. "Have you got a knitting needle?" he asked.

Trying not to show her surprise,

Megan said, "No, I haven't, but I'm sure Sister Moore has got some in the drawer of her desk. She often knits at night when things are quiet."

"I'm not asking for the history of the knitting needle, just get me one," snapped Giles bad-temperedly.

Megan glowered at him. No need to snap my head off like that, she thought rebelliously, having to remind herself that he was trying to help her and that really she should be grateful. "Do you want any particular number?" she asked.

"I only want one," he said.

"I mean any particular size," repeated Megan, thinking how ridiculous their conversation must sound.

"The smallest, thinnest one you can get," he replied.

Luckily Juliet Moore had quite a supply in her drawer.

"Don't tell him I've got all these," she said as she searched for the smallest one. "Otherwise he'll think I never do anything but knit all night!"

"I shouldn't worry about that," replied Megan. "If he gets too objectionable you could always stab him with one of these spare needles." She made a vicious lunging movement through the air.

Juliet raised her eyebrows. "I thought you liked him," she said.

"I'm off him," said Megan forcefully. Then she paused on her way out of the door. "Not, of course, that I ever really liked him," she added.

Juliet Moore just smiled as she closed the drawer of her desk and said nothing, leaving Megan knowing, as she made her way back to the seminar room armed with the knitting needle, that she had not convinced her in the slightest!

She silently handed Giles the needle, although what purpose he had in mind for it she just couldn't imagine.

"Ah," he said, taking it from her, "just the right size. Now I'm sure this will do the trick." He slotted the needle through where the screw should go and then, with the aid of his wedge of paper, managed to manoeuvre the magnifying glass to the right place and gently let go of it. The glass stayed in place, reflecting Megan's transparency perfectly on to the screen on the wall.

Giles put his hands in the pockets of his white coat with a sigh of satisfaction. "There you are, just shows what a little ingenuity can do," he said. "With the aid of a piece of paper and a knitting needle the projector is fixed."

"The marvels of modern science," said Megan with a little laugh. "Thank you very much, and now I've got to practise my lecture for tomorrow." She turned away and picked up her notes. "Goodnight, thanks again for helping me out."

"Don't mention it," said Giles, not moving. "Have you . . . " He hesitated. "Have you seen any jobs you like advertised yet?"

"I haven't had time to look," said Megan, keeping her head lowered over her notes. "Today has been very busy.

I'll probably flick through the journals tonight when I've finished here."

"Joanna starts at her new school the day after tomorrow," he said, still not moving.

"I know," answered Megan stiffly, wishing he would go. Awkwardly she shuffled the papers in her hand and one page floated out from the sheaf and drifted down on to the floor. They both bent down to pick it up simultaneously and their hands touched as they went to grasp it. No amount of self-control could stop the shivering sensation that swept through Megan at the touch of his hand. Her heart quickened its beat, sending a flood of warmth stealing through her veins.

"Megan, I . . . " he began.

"Please excuse me, but I really must run through this lecture and I'm very tired," said Megan quickly. It was a dismissal and he knew it. "Thank you once again for fixing the projector for me," she said, stiffly polite, "it was very kind of you."

"That's quite all right," replied Giles in exactly the same tone of voice as he stood up. Then he turned swiftly on his heel and walked out of the seminar room door.

Megan watched his departing figure with a deep feeling of despair engulfing her. She would have to leave; she couldn't bear being so close to him. She wanted him for herself and herself alone, and bitterly she had to acknowledge that it could never be like that.

She ran through her lecture automatically, hardly knowing what she was saying, and when she had finished she neatly stacked up her notes and transparencies, switched off the lights, locked the room and went back to the nurses' block. She felt totally drained of emotion, like a robot, except for the nagging pain in her heart.

Next day her lecture went off smoothly. The overhead projector stayed in one piece, thanks to Giles' ingenuity, and by the end of the one and a half hour period Megan felt quite pleased with herself. Only her unhappiness about Giles marred the morning, but that was something she'd have to learn to live with, she told herself. She didn't see him at all that morning and she knew he would be away in the afternoon, for he would be taking Joanna and her trunks to her new boarding school.

On impulse Megan rang the number of his hospital flat from her office to say goodbye and good luck to Joanna. She had just seen a back view of Giles disappearing down the corridor with one of the orthopaedic surgeons so she guessed he would not be going back to the flat right away.

Joanna answered the telephone. "Hello," she said cautiously, "Joanna Elliott speaking."

"It's Megan," said Megan. "I'm sorry I haven't been able to see you again before you go off to school, but I just rang to wish you good luck and to say I hope you'll be happy there."

"Thanks," Joanna's voice brightened on the other end of the line. "It's nice of you to ring. In fact I'm glad you have, because I've been worried."

"Worried?" asked Megan softly. "Surely you're not worried about your new school? You can take it from the horse's mouth, you are going to have a great time there. Two years will pass before you know it, and then you will be really grown up, going to university or doing something equally exciting."

"It's not me I'm worried about," said Joanna, "it's you."

"Me?" echoed Megan in astonishment.

"Well, not just you," said Joanna, "you and Dad. I thought, well . . . I know Dad thinks a lot of you, and I thought perhaps you and he . . . " Her voice trailed off.

"Joanna, you are not having romantic dreams again, are you?" asked Megan. "I've told you before you should let your father sort out his own life."

"Well, he doesn't seem to be making a very good job of it," replied Joanna stubbornly, "and now the problem of me has been settled there is no excuse."

"Oh, Joanna," sighed Megan, "life isn't as simple as you would like it to be, or as I would like it to be either, come to that." She paused for a moment, then said, "I know perhaps you don't like your Aunt Fiona much, but has it occurred to you that perhaps your father has special feelings for her — perhaps even loves her?"

Joanna burst out laughing. "I sincerely hope not!" she snorted. "She has been happily married to the most odiously rich man for the last ten years, and I have two absolutely horrible little cousins. That was why I didn't want to spend my last two years of school in the States. I would have had to live with my cousins all the time, and they are so American I just can't stand them." She laughed again. "They're not exactly overfond of me, either."

Megan sat on the edge of her desk in the office holding the phone against her ear as if in a trance — she was absolutely dumbfounded. Giles had never mentioned that Fiona was married, but that still didn't account for him telling her that he shouldn't have kissed her, and that he succumbed to attractive women too easily.

"Megan, are you still there?" asked Joanna's voice at the other end of the line.

"Yes, yes," stammered Megan, "I'm still here."

She heard Joanna draw a deep breath, then she said, "I know Dad is going to shoot me for saying this, but I think he is afraid."

"Afraid?" echoed Megan weakly.

"Yes, afraid," said Joanna firmly. "He's afraid that someone as young and beautiful as you will turn him down, so he has steered away from you, afraid to commit himself. Men are like that," she added wisely, "too proud. Once they've been hurt they are afraid of being hurt again, and so end up not taking any risks at all."

Megan found her voice at last. "For

a sixteen-year-old you have some very interesting theories," she said slowly.

"Promise me you'll be nice to him," insisted Joanna quickly. "Give him a chance."

Megan smiled; she felt as if her room was filled with blinding sunlight, such a burden had been lifted from her shoulders. "I promise, Joanna," she said softly.

The rest of the day passed for Megan as if in a dream. Yes, she would be nice to him when she saw him next. In fact, she decided, she would kick away any traces of her pride and fling herself at him. If he rebuffs you, that's that she told herself. But now she knew he was free she just had to find out how he really felt about her. Was he prepared to commit himself?

Thursday morning can't go quickly enough, thought Megan as she got ready for duty the following day. It would be hard to wait until Giles came back and was on duty again in the afternoon, but wait she would have to.

However, just ten minutes after she had reported for duty that morning, pandemonium broke out. The hospital went on red alert, for there had been a serious coach accident on the motorway and the nearest exit point for transporting the victims to was the County General. The first casualties started arriving just ten minutes after the alert had been received and the staff of the casualty department slipped into their "major incident' roles like impeccably rehearsed actors. Megan was amazed at the smoothness and the calm which everyone portrayed. They had often rehearsed a major incident, but had never actually had to deal with a real one.

The coach that had crashed had been full of old-age pensioners on an outing and there was a formidable range of injuries. All thoughts of Giles Elliott were wiped from her mind as Megan struggled along with the rest of the team, plus the off-duty staff who came back into the hospital to help. The casualties were sorted by the senior surgical registrar into three categories, the most serious of which went straight up to the general theatres on the next floor. The less serious injuries were dealt with in the operating theatre attached to the casualty unit, and those suffering from shock and minor injuries were helped in the accident waiting area.

Megan was part of the team dealing with injuries in the theatre. There was an intense atmosphere, but not one of panic, as everyone worked methodically and as quickly as possible to help the patients. Megan was impressed by the fortitude and courage shown by the old people; not one of them complained and all were pathetically grateful.

She helped the pupil nurse clean up the theatre quickly after they had just finished suturing an old woman's hand, and then they were ready to receive the next patient, an elderly man in a very shocked condition with badly lacerated legs. He had lost a lot of blood and was weak and faint.

"He ought to be transferred to the upstairs theatres really," said the surgical registrar as he cut away the old man's trouser leg.

"I know," said Megan watching anxiously, "but I've checked to see, and they are doing a ruptured spleen up there at the moment, so it's all hands on deck and they don't know when they are going to finish." As she spoke she noticed the blanket covering the upper half of the old man move.

"Don't worry," she said, gently placing her hand on the patient's chest, "everything is going to be all right, I promise. You are in good hands now."

The old man opened his pale watery blue eyes. "It's Minnie," he whispered.

"Minnie?" said Megan. "Who is Minnie? Tell me where she is and I'll make sure she knows you are going to be all right."

"Minnie's here," he whispered weakly, nodding towards the blanket covering his chest.

Gently Megan pulled back the blanket to be confronted by the frightened gaze of a tiny Yorkshire terrier. He must have held her all through the horrific crash and kept her with him ever since.

"Don't let her die," he pleaded.

"What's that?" asked the surgeon, trying to clean the wounds before he decided what he needed to do. "Is the anaesthetist ready yet? We ought to get started."

"Nurse, come here a moment," Megan said quietly to the staff nurse standing on the other side of the table. Gently she reached forward and took the small dog in her arms. "Don't worry about Minnie, Mr Jackson," she said after quickly reading the label with his name on it. "I'll take good care of her until you are better, I give you my word." She turned quickly to the staff nurse. "I'll just go and put this little dog safely in my office, then I'll scrub up again and be back. Will you be OK here for a moment?"

Staff nodded, her eyes wide in astonishment at the sight of the little dog. Megan took the opportunity of the surgeon's preoccupation with the leg wounds to make her escape from theatre with Minnie in her arms. She hurried down the corridor, the little quivering dog held against her, and when she reached her office she made a little bed for it in one of the drawers by putting a blanket in it. Then she put a saucer of water by the side of the drawer.

"There you are, Minnie," she said softly, "I'm afraid I'm going to have to leave you there until we have your master sorted out." She locked the office door behind her when she left; it would never do for Minnie to escape and get lost, not after she had promised old Mr Jackson that she would take good care of her.

Once back in theatre her mind returned to the task in hand. Mr Jackson was given a blood transfusion, had his lacerated legs sutured neatly by the surgeon and was then transferred to one of the upstairs wards.

Almost all the casualties had been cleared and the accident and emergency team were looking forward to a well-earned coffee-break when suddenly the fire alarm bells started. There were only a few patients left in the waiting area and they were about to be taken back home by ambulance; otherwise, apart from staff, the area was clear.

The patients were put quickly aboard the waiting ambulance. No one took any undue notice of the fire alarm; the fire bells were always ringing and it was always a false alarm.

"I don't know why they don't get those electronic things that set those bells off fixed somehow," grumbled one of the ambulance men as he helped an old lady into the ambulance.

Megan agreed. "The trouble is, if there ever really is a fire," she said, "none of us will take any notice."

"Wait until the smoke starts coming, that's my motto," joked the ambulance man. Megan was inclined to agree with him. The bells were still ringing as she made her way back from the ambulance bay into Casualty. She glanced at her watch; almost two o'clock and Giles Elliott should be on duty soon. Her heart throbbed in anticipation of seeing him again. She began to walk slowly past the now empty cubicles towards her office when she heard the explosion, and then suddenly a great pall of acrid black smoke rolled like a ball down the corridor towards her. At the same time she heard the crackle of flames and felt the heat from the smoke as it engulfed her.

The surgical registrar she had been helping in theatre ran past her, grabbing her as he ran, a staff nurse and a pupil nurse with him.

"There has been an explosion of some sort in the X-ray department," he shouted. "I think the rubber cabling has caught fire. Come on, before we all choke."

Once outside, one of the staff nurses,

who was the designated safety officer for the casualty area, quickly lined up the staff and counted them.

"Thank God everyone is here," she said with a sigh of relief.

"Thank God it didn't happen when we had all those casualties in from the coach," said the surgical registrar soberly.

It was then that Megan remembered Minnie, who was still locked up in her office. She thought quickly. If the surgical registrar was right, and the fire was in the X-ray department, that was some way from her office. The only problem was breathing in that thick black smoke.

She had a spare theatre mask in her apron pocket and hastily putting it on she dashed back into the building. The others tried to stop her, but Megan dodged them. The old man's pleading eyes haunted her — she couldn't let Minnie die, not without trying to save her.

Once inside the building the smoke

was worse than Megan had thought, thick black and choking. She found it almost impossible to see and could feel the heat from the flames which she could now sense at the end of the corridor.

Desperately she made her way along, holding on to the wall so that she wouldn't lose her sense of direction, her eyes half-closed to the acrid smoke and fumes. She reached the door of her office safely and fumbled to get the key in the lock. It wouldn't go in. Feverishly she felt for the keyhole, unable to open her eyes to see properly. There was another explosion and a sheet of brilliant orange flame shot down the corridor, the tongues licking the floor only a few feet from where Megan stood. "Please, please let me open the door," she prayed out loud. Then the key slid into the lock and she turned it and went into her office. The room was relatively smoke free for a second as she opened the door, just long enough for her to see Minnie, still sitting on the blanket and looking very frightened.

Quickly Megan picked her up. The little dog coughed and spluttered as the thick smoke swirled around them. Megan hesitated for a moment, then took off her mask and tied it around the dog's face, covering her tiny nose and mouth, and the huge, frightened eyes. I've got enough sense to hold my breath, she thought as she started back, but Minnie hasn't. She knew the tiny creature would be asphyxiated very easily, for her lungs were only small. Megan just prayed that she would be able to hold her breath for long enough to get out.

She made her way back towards the faint light of day at the far end of the corridor, which indicated the exit from Casualty to the safety of the outside. She traced her way along the wall with one hand and held on to Minnie tightly with the other. The daylight seemed so far away; Megan felt her head beginning to swim and knew she would have to take a breath soon, but she also knew that if she started breathing in that black smoke she would soon lose consciousness.

Falteringly she made her way along. The daylight seemed to be as far away as ever, would she ever reach it? There was another explosion and she felt the searing heat scorching her back. Then, in the murky darkness, she tripped over a chair and went sprawling and the inevitable happened — she took a breath. The acrid smoke filled her lungs and she started coughing in an uncontrollable spasm, but she never once let go her tight hold of Minnie, who by now was a terrified wriggling bundle in her arms. I'm going to die, was her last conscious thought. Then she felt herself being lifted up and she floated into unconsciousness.

The muted sound of voices eddied around her. It was as if she was in a deep pool and was slowly surfacing. Dimly she was aware of Giles' face above her, looking anxious. Why is he worrying, thought Megan dreamily — everything is all right. Minnie is safe and that's the most important thing . . .

It was the thought of Minnie that jolted her back into consciousness and she sat up abruptly. "Where's Minnie?" she demanded.

"Do you mean that scrap of fur you risked your life for?" asked Giles, his voice grim, motioning to the attending nurse to leave the room.

"She's not just a scrap of fur, she's an old man's pet," answered Megan, adding anxiously, "Where is she?"

Giles sat on the edge of the bed and Megan suddenly realised that she was in a small side room off of one of the upstairs wards. "That wretched animal is doing fine in my room," he said. "She's eaten a tin of the most expensive dog food and drunk a saucer of milk. Now, does that satisfy you?"

Megan sank back among the pillows, her eyes filled with tears. "Yes, thank you," she whispered. "I couldn't have borne it if anything had happened to her. I promised Mr Jackson I would look after her and he would be so alone without her." She shuddered at the memory of that ghastly floundering journey through the black smoke. "I don't remember walking out," she said.

"You didn't," said Giles grimly. "A fireman and I got you out just in time. You had fallen unconscious, overcome by smoke. What on earth possessed you to go without a mask at least?"

"The dog needed it," said Megan. "Her lungs are smaller than mine and I thought she would suffocate first."

Giles sighed. "That was an incredibly stupid thing to do," he said. Then his grim mouth relaxed a little. "But an incredibly brave thing too, and unselfish. Perhaps you're not the hard woman you've tried to convince me you were."

Megan looked at him sitting there on the edge of her bed. She felt more awake now — awake enough to know she was wearing a flimsy cotton hospital nightgown which clung to the firm contours of her young body. Self-consciously she tugged the sheets up around her shoulders. "How long have I been here?" she asked, her voice faltering.

"Twenty-four hours," said Giles huskily. "Twenty-four hours in which I've had plenty of time to think."

"Oh," said Megan uncertainly, the look in his blue eyes sending prickles of apprehension up and down her spine. "What have you been thinking about?" she whispered.

"Us," he said quietly. Then his sculptured lips relaxed and curved into a tender smile as he bent towards her. He lifted her, unresisting, from the austere hospital bed and cradled her in his arms, sliding his warm hands beneath the straps of the hospital gown until they rested possessively against her soft flesh.

"When you were in that burning building I thought I'd never see you again," he whispered against her hair.

"I knew what I've been trying to deny to myself ever since I first met you. I knew that I loved you, and that I can't live without you." He shuddered suddenly and held her closer. "And I almost lost you."

Megan pushed him away a little to look at him, then she grinned impishly. "You couldn't lose someone like me," she said. "I'll always turn up like the proverbial bad penny."

"Oh, Megan," he whispered, "you are my *good* penny. Tell me that you care for me, just a little."

For an answer Megan linked her arms around his head and drew his face down to hers. Eagerly her soft, trembling mouth sought out his and eagerly too he responded, his warm lips moving persuasively over hers. She kissed him back passionately, impulsively, all the pent-up feelings of the last few months released at last. Finally Giles pulled away from her and his lips tingled a path down her throat towards the madly pulsating hollow of her throat.

"Say it," he commanded, his voice hoarse with emotion.

"What do you want me to say?" whispered Megan.

"Just three little words will do for a start," he said. "I love you."

"I love you," whispered back Megan dutifully. Then she confessed, "I've loved you for a long time, but I thought . . ." Her voice trailed away. It seemed silly to mention it now.

"I know, Joanna told me. You thought I was enamoured or attached in some way to Fiona," he said. Then he raised he head and gazed down at Megan with his brilliant blue eyes. "I was married when I was very young. It was disastrous from the very beginning and the only good thing that came out of the union was Joanna. If it hadn't been for her I would never have had to have stayed in close contact with Fiona." He sighed. "I've got to explain this to you — I don't want any misunderstandings. Fiona and I agreed that we would meet every year until Joanna was sixteen; then Joanna would go and live with her for two years until she was eighteen. We had to do this because of a trust fund which we had to administer jointly for Joanna. I'm afraid Fiona and I never agreed on how it should be administered, but now at last we have come to an amicable agreement and everything has been sorted out. Joanna will stay here, the money will be inherited by her when she is eighteen, and I need never see Fiona again."

He drew Megan to him tightly. "Now that at last everything has been sorted out, I feel free to ask you the most important thing of all."

"What is that?" whispered Megan against the warmth of his neck.

"Will you marry me? I think it should be as soon as possible, I need to be put out of my misery."

"But are you sure this is the right thing to do?" Megan half teased. "Don't you think we should give ourselves more time?"

"I certainly do not think time is indicated," said Giles as his mouth came down on hers with unrelenting passion. "And remember, Doctor knows best!"

When at last she surfaced from his passionate onslaught Megan just had the strength to whisper contentedly, "Yes, Doctor."

"You won't change your mind and decide your career is more important, and that I would be standing in your way?" he demanded.

"You can stand in my way any time," breathed Megan, drawing his face closer to hers.

"I warn you," said Giles, the weight of his body pressing her back among the pillows, "I shall be there all the time."

WITH SOMEBODY ELSE
Theresa Charles

Rosamond sets off for Cornwall with Hugo to meet his family, blissfully unaware of the shocks in store for her.

A SUMMER FOR STRANGERS
Claire Hamilton

Because she had lost her job, her flat and she had no money, Tabitha agreed to pose as Adam's future wife although she believed the scheme to be deceitful and cruel.

VILLA OF SINGING WATER
Angela Petron

The disquieting incidents that occurred at the Vatican and the Colosseum did not trouble Jan at first, but then they became increasingly unpleasant and alarming.

DOCTOR NAPIER'S NURSE
Pauline Ash

When cousins Midge and Derry are entered as probationer nurses on the same day but at different hospitals they agree to exchange identities.

A GIRL LIKE JULIE
Louise Ellis

Caroline absolutely adored Hugh Barrington, but then Julie Crane came into their lives. Julie was the kind of girl who attracts men without even trying.

COUNTRY DOCTOR
Paula Lindsay

When Evan Richmond bought a practice in a remote country village he did not realise that a casual encounter would lead to the loss of his heart.

ENCORE
Helga Moray

Craig and Janet realise that their true happiness lies with each other, but it is only under traumatic circumstances that they can be reunited.

NICOLETTE
Ivy Preston

When Grant Alston came back into her life, Nicolette was faced with a dilemma. Should she follow the path of duty or the path of love?

THE GOLDEN PUMA
Margaret Way

Catherine's time was spent looking after her father's Queensland farm. But what life was there without David, who wasn't interested in her?

HOSPITAL BY THE LAKE
Anne Durham

Nurse Marguerite Ingleby was always ready to become personally involved with her patients, to the despair of Brian Field, the Senior Surgical Registrar, who loved her.

VALLEY OF CONFLICT
David Farrell

Isolated in a hostel in the French Alps, Ann Russell sees her fiancé being seduced by a young girl. Then comes the avalanche that imperils their lives.

NURSE'S CHOICE
Peggy Gaddis

A proposal of marriage from the incredibly handsome and wealthy Reagan was enough to upset any girl — and Brooke Martin was no exception.

A DANGEROUS MAN
Anne Goring

Photographer Polly Burton was on safari in Mombasa when she met enigmatic Leon Hammond. But unpredictability was the name of the game where Leon was concerned.

PRECIOUS INHERITANCE
Joan Moules

Karen's new life working for an authoress took her from Sussex to a foreign airstrip and a kidnapping; to a real life adventure as gripping as any in the books she typed.

VISION OF LOVE
Grace Richmond

When Kathy takes over the rundown country kennels she finds Alec Stinton, a local vet, very helpful. But their friendship arouses bitter jealousy and a tragedy seems inevitable.

CRUSADING NURSE
Jane Converse

It was handsome Dr. Corbett who opened Nurse Susan Leighton's eyes and who set her off on a lonely crusade against some powerful enemies and a shattering struggle against the man she loved.

WILD ENCHANTMENT
Christina Green

Rowan's agreeable new boss had a dream of creating a famous perfume using her precious Silverstar, but Rowan's plans were very different.

DESERT ROMANCE
Irene Ord

Sally agrees to take her sister Pam's place as La Chartreuse, the dancer, but she finds out there is more to it than dyeing her hair red and looking like her sister.

HEART OF ICE
Marie Sidney

How was January to know that not only would the warmth of the Swiss people thaw out her frozen heart, but that she too would play her part in helping someone to live again?

LUCKY IN LOVE
Margaret Wood

Companion-secretary to wealthy gambler Laura Duxford, who lived in Monaco, seemed to Melanie a fabulous job. Especially as Melanie had already lost her heart to Laura's son, Julian.

NURSE TO PRINCESS JASMINE
Lilian Woodward

Nick's surgeon brother, Tom, performs an operation on an Arabian princess, and she invites Tom, Nick and his fiancé to Omander, where a web of deceit and intrigue closes about them.

THE WAYWARD HEART
Eileen Barry

Disaster-prone Katherine's nickname was "Kate Calamity", but her boss went too far with an outrageous proposal, which because of her latest disaster, she could not refuse.

FOUR WEEKS IN WINTER
Jane Donnelly

Tessa wasn't looking forward to meeting Paul Mellor again — she had made a fool of herself over him once before. But was Orme Jared's solution to her problem likely to be the right one?

SURGERY BY THE SEA
Sheila Douglas

Medical student Meg hadn't really wanted to go and work with a G.P. on the Welsh coast although the job had its compensations. But Owen Roberts was certainly not one of them!

HEAVEN IS HIGH
Anne Hampson

The new heir to the Manor of Marbeck had been found. But it was rather unfortunate that when he arrived unexpectedly he found an uninvited guest, complete with stetson and high boots.

LOVE WILL COME
Sarah Devon

June Baker's boss was not really her idea of her ideal man, but when she went from third typist to boss's secretary overnight she began to change her mind.

ESCAPE TO ROMANCE
Kay Winchester

Oliver and Jean first met on Swale Island. They were both trying to begin their lives afresh, but neither had bargained for complications from the past.

CASTLE IN THE SUN
Cora Mayne

Emma's invalid sister, Kym, needed a warm climate, and Emma jumped at the chance of a job on a Mediterranean island. But Emma soon finds that intrigues and hazards lurk on the sunlit isle.

BEWARE OF LOVE
Kay Winchester

Carol Brampton resumes her nursing career when her family is killed in a car accident. With Dr. Patrick Farrell she begins to pick up the pieces of her life, but is bitterly hurt when insinuations are made about her to Patrick.

DARLING REBEL
Sarah Devon

When Jason Farradale's secretary met with an accident, her glamorous stand-in was quite unable to deal with one problem in particular.